A CANDLELIGHT ROMANCE

CANDLELIGHT ROMANCES

MAN
IN A
MILLION

ROWENA WILSON

A Candlelight Romance

Published by
Dell Publishing Co., Inc.
1 Dag Hammarskjold Plaza
New York, New York 10017

Dell ® TM 681510, Dell Publishing Co., Inc.

ISBN: 0–440–15528–2

Printed in the United States of America
First printing—July 1981

CHAPTER ONE

It was raining when Jasmine arrived in Toronto. The flight had been singularly unspectacular and Jasmine, who had been looking forward to her first transatlantic flight, had felt her heart as heavy as the clouds which had surrounded the plane, threatening, it seemed, almost to engulf it and swallow it up.

The unhappy immobility of her face had attracted the curiosity of the young man next to her on the plane, and he had valiantly tried to draw her out of herself into a friendly conversation. But all to no avail. Jasmine had steadfastly and coolly repelled all his advances. *He wouldn't even notice my existence if Janice were sitting in the other seat next to him,* she thought mutinously, unconsciously blaming the innocent stranger for some deep-rooted trauma that was certainly none of his making.

Janice! Why was the mere thought of her twin enough to reduce Jasmine to self-criticism and dissatisfaction? Why did she always feel so totally overwhelmed and overshadowed by Janice? But even as she asked herself the question, Jasmine knew in her heart the answer. How could two identical twins be so basically and so distinctly unalike? It was true that they were so similar both in looks and in name that people often mistook one for the other; but it was what Janice did with her looks that made the difference.

Janice knew how to attract, to glow, to mesmerize. How often had her twin discovered that to her disadvantage! How often had Jasmine taken home some particularly interested young man only to see his interest in her fade the minute Janice came on the scene. Oh, how that hurt! To be loved and admired for oneself just as long as dear twin sister remained out of the way!

And yet she found she couldn't honestly blame men for hanging adoringly around Janice, who knew only too well how to show off her charms to advantage. Janice and Jasmine were in fact carbon copies of each other until a member of the male species arrived on the scene, and then an amazing change would come over Janice; her pretty lips would blossom into a pout and her gray eyes would become limpid pools with smoky depths.

"Oh, how I envy her!" sighed Jasmine as she stirred in the narrow seat and glowered at the man beside her, who was by this time immersed in a novel. Quite unfairly (for, after all, he had tried to talk to her and had been repulsed) she thought, *Now, there's a perfect example of the difference between us. If I were Janice, that young man would be totally engrossed in me, laughing, smiling and feeling on top of the world because he's an attractive man sitting next to a beautiful woman! Well, I don't care!*

But she did.

Her resentment of her twin only made her feel worse, for she was basically a very generous and loving person, and resentment made her feel guilty. She would atone, she decided. She would atone by making a really determined effort to find Janice who, it appeared, had arrived in Canada some six months ago, had written one postcard full of praise for the country and the people, particularly those people in a little place called Lion's Head, and had promptly disappeared. Or, at least, she hadn't bothered to communicate further with her family in England, a family so frantic with worry by now that they had sent Jasmine in search of her errant twin.

The rain in Toronto did nothing to dispel Jasmine's gloomy mood. Eight o'clock in the morning was a dismal time to arrive anywhere, and why on earth had she not made inquiries and more definite arrangements before leaving England?

If I'm not careful, she thought ruefully, *I'll end up as lost as Janice.*

How did one get to Lion's Head, and where was it? As she stood undecidedly looking around her, she glimpsed through the crowd a booth and a sign: HERTZ RENT-A-CAR. Breathing a sigh of relief, she picked up her valise and walked in that direction.

Half an hour later, armed with a road map, a sheaf of information, and a key to one of the smaller varieties of American cars, she walked across the airport parking lot.

"If I ever find my way, it'll be a miracle," she muttered to herself as she swung the nimble vehicle out of the parking lot and into the Canadian freeway traffic. Much to her delight she found that the little car responded readily to her every command, and after a few miles she even felt quite comfortable driving on the right-hand side of the road.

The rental people had assured her that finding her way to Lion's Head in the Bruce Peninsula would be a breeze—even taking into account her complete ineptitude at map reading! She followed Highway 10 to Orangeville successfully enough, and at Shelbourne ascertained that she was indeed on the right road and that all she had to do was to drive northward until she reached Owen Sound.

All this she accomplished successfully, not through any particular skill, but because there were in fact very few other roads to follow anyway. But at about the same time that she hit Owen Sound, so did a freak winter storm.

Looking back in retrospect she just didn't see how it could have taken her so unawares. She supposed that to a native used to noting the signs of the weather the steadily increasing winds would have meant something. She must admit that she had noticed a tugging on the steering wheel, and she had admired the exaggerated dipping of the winter skeletons of trees, but it had never occurred to her that this was the forewarning of a storm of maniacal force.

Jasmine was glad at least that by the time the first snowflakes had started to fall she had negotiated the little car through the town and on to the road to the Bruce Peninsula. She knew by a glance at the map that all she had to do was to drive straight ahead to Wiarton, and then twenty miles onto the peninsula she would see a turnoff pointing to Lion's Head. What she intended to do when she got there, or where she intended to stay, she had no idea. But that was scarcely her most pressing concern at the moment.

Later she couldn't remember how she had completed the last part of the journey. The fright of it receded into the mists of her mind and she was glad of that. The snow increased to such an extent that even with the windshield wipers at their fastest speed the windows were never completely clear of snow. At every moment she expected the car to crunch down a hidden embankment at the side of the road. She was terrified that in the poor visibility she would miss a crossroads or some traffic lights, or run into a car looming too suddenly out of the white curtain in the opposite direction.

It seemed hours later when she reached a fork in the road with a signpost so nearly obliterated by the snow that she could not read the wording. But by this time she was past caring where she ended up. All she wanted was shelter—four walls around her to shield her from the storm and cut out that frightful shrieking of the wind. The road ahead began to twist and turn and climb all at once so that now she had the impression that she was heading into some wild no-man's-land ruled by the howling elements and the wild beasts. The snow was falling so thick and fast that her little car's windshield wipers began to labor under the strain and she found that she had to stop every five minutes or so to clear the clogged snow out of them.

Once she had begun to think of wild beasts it took a superhuman effort to open the car door and to actually step out into the storm's fury. And fury it was. The storm was blowing from behind her so that it was easy to open the car door. In fact it flew out of her restraining hand the minute she released the catch, and when she stepped out of the car the wind wrapped itself around her and carried her off with such force that she had to hold on to the door so as not to be swept away.

The harshness of the wind grated at her lungs, and by the time she had struggled back to the safety of the interior of the car she was half weeping, and the sound of her rasping breath frightened her in the darkness. Three times she ventured out to free the wipers, and then even that became unnecessary as she realized that the drifts on the road were so deep that her car could no longer negotiate them. Actually she had no idea if she was still on the road or not. She could see around her nothing but whiteness. The howling wind delighted in her plight and mercilessly buffeted the car.

Panic-stricken, Jasmine wondered which was the lesser of two evils—to stay in the car and risk freezing to death, or to go out and look for shelter where there likely was none. If she stayed in the car with the engine running for warmth, she would stand a good chance of being overcome by carbon monoxide fumes. And yet how far would she get walking in this blizzard?

All these thoughts flitted indecisively through her mind, and then she became aware of a flashing light to the left through intermittent swirls of snow. Could it be a house? A car?

Recklessly she lurched out of the car and struggled forward against the wind toward the flickering light.

The house loomed suddenly out of the white blizzard, a dark sinister mass which gave her such a scare that her progress was momentarily checked. But, after all, there was nowhere else for her to go. She was forced to seek refuge there or face certain death in the snow. Sinister though the house appeared, she knew at least there were people there. That much was obvious from the several cars crouched in the swirling snow around the house like empty-eyed gargoyles waiting to pounce on their prey.

The last twenty yards to the door were the longest of all. The wind whipped the loose snow into excited clouds. Jasmine's breath rasped in her chest and rattled in her throat. She tried to cover her mouth with her coat collar, but by this time she was sobbing and shaking so uncontrollably that she knew that if she didn't make the shelter of the doorway soon she was going to sink down into the protection of the banked snow and give herself up to hopeless oblivion.

She never knew afterward what gave her that superhuman strength to climb the steps to the door, but she suspected that she had put too small a price on life until it seemed likely to be snatched away from her. As she fought her way to the door, her face raw and lashed by the icy wind, her legs crippled by the cold and the restraining snowdrifts, she had some crazy idea that she was about to be cheated out of life before she had even lived it.

Well, she wasn't going to be cheated that easily!

She pounded, sobbing, on the door and got no answer. Again she hammered in desperation with the same result. She leaned against the door, tears of frustration coursing down her cheeks and melting little channels in the ice coating her face. Then the door suddenly opened, sending her sprawling into a brightly lit hallway and the warmth of somebody's arms! Her overall impression at that moment was of welcome and security after the bitter cold of the storm outside.

Maybe that's why she clung foolishly a little longer than necessary, her face against a silk shirt that smelled faintly, elusively of Brut.

She would probably have stayed there a good while longer if the arms hadn't slackened. In contrast to their previous gentleness the two hands gripped her shoulders roughly and held her at arm's length. She could hardly believe her ears.

"So you've come back at last, Janice!" The harsh voice matched the rough hands that trembled as though they would like to shake her or maybe even snap her in two. "Not a moment too soon, either! You won't escape again so easily!"

Even as she opened her mouth to deny the identity so hastily thrust upon her, some inner caution made Jasmine quickly—albeit half-guiltily—change her mind. She would play along with it for a while and see if she could unearth some clue as to her sister's whereabouts.

She took a deep breath and raised her eyes. How dared he speak to her in that tone of voice! She could well imagine why Janice had run away—as it seemed

12

she had—from this monster! She shuddered as her eyes met his, and then hers fell, unable to bear the scorn and cruelty mirrored there.

The man towering over her was handsome even in his rage. His hair was of such a dark ash color that it gave the impression that he was black-haired, save for the patches where the light played on the silvery tendrils curling around his ears and forehead. The eyes blazing at her now were of the most vivid green she had ever seen, and seemed to be lit from within, such was their luminous quality—like a wildcat's in the darkness of the forest, Jasmine thought, trying to suppress the drumming of her heart.

"You're hurting me!" she informed him, wishing her voice wouldn't break as though on the brink of childish tears.

She disengaged herself, took a step back, and bravely tried to outstare those hypnotic eyes.

It was then that she noticed that his mouth was not at all hard and cruel as she had first suspected, but rather soft and full. In fact, if she was not much mistaken, it was even beginning to curve into a smile.

"Well, well! No tears and tantrums this time?" He moved away from her toward a well-equipped bar. "No pretty pouting displays?" He looked searchingly at her. "This indeed is a new Janice—a mutinous child!" He dismissed her, leaving her standing in a puddle of water rapidly forming from the ice on her clothing, and he busied himself at the bar.

Jasmine looked around her with interest. The wide entrance door led straight into a large room that was at once entrance hall and receiving lounge. The walls were oak paneled and hung with tapestries and paintings of animals; the ceilings rose high into beamed vaults. To her immediate left was an ornate type of tallboy, set into the wall, on which hung an assortment of outdoor garments, and directly ahead of her at the far end of the room, a wide staircase curved upward and out of sight. The furniture was heavy and solidly comfortable and the floor was richly covered in a plush carpet of vivid autumn hues. The most welcome sight of all in her present state was the wide stone fireplace in the center, the chimney thrusting up into the roof some thirty feet above. How she longed for the warmth and comfort of the fire to cast the chill from her icy bones! How weary she felt, and how afraid! It occurred to her that she might be letting herself in for more than she bargained for. Her eyes returned to the stranger. It would be madness to stay here. Better not start to play this dangerously deceitful game.

The room was doing funny things, tipping and tilting like some fairground ride. The walls advanced and receded and, as the floor came up to meet her shocked gaze, she felt two strong arms swiftly scoop her up and carry her over to the fireplace where she was gently lowered on to a soft warm chesterfield. She felt gentle hands removing first her boots and coat and then rubbing her frozen feet.

Embarrassment brought her to her senses and she struggled away, a flush staining her cheeks.

"I—I'm all right now, thank you!" she gulped. "I don't know what made me do that."

If he noticed her confusion, he didn't show it.

"No doubt the sudden change from icy cold to heat," he murmured, taking her hand and curling her fingers around a glass containing a bronze-colored liquid. "Brandy for you this time instead of your favorite. It will do you more good."

Seeing the question in her eyes he laughed shortly. "Oh, come now, Janice, you may have been gone for over two months, but I do still remember your favorite drink is crème de menthe."

Of course! It was Janice's favorite. Jasmine carefully reminded herself that she would have to remember that, now she was supposed to be her sister, she would have to act like Janice and think like Janice or her little game would be soon found out.

Nevertheless she did not know what to do or say in her situation. Her sister had written nothing about this aspect of her stay in Canada. Why, she didn't even know the name of this handsome specimen. And handsome he was. Trust Janice to pick one like this, thought Jasmine with a flash of envy.

Not knowing what to say, she sat twirling her glass and enjoying little sips of the warm liquid, all the while taking surreptitious glances at the man at her side, noting the smooth lithe way he got up and crossed the room to the bar to fetch his own drink.

Her pleasant moment of peace was short-lived, however. He returned to sit in the wing chair on the other side of the fireplace, lazily stretching his feet out in front of him.

"Okay, Janice. Let's have it!"

Her heart thudded sickeningly in her chest and a drop of brandy spilled onto her dress. That gained

15

her a moment of time as she pretended to scrub busily at the spot.

He was unimpressed.

"I'm waiting, Janice." It was quietly said, but that made it all the more threatening.

There was nothing to do but try to bluff it out.

She raised her eyes defiantly to look at him. "Then you're going to wait a long time because I have nothing to say!"

She thought the roof was going to erupt.

"Nothing to say? Just like that? *Nothing to say?*" He sprang to his feet and took a step toward her as though about to pounce on her and tear her apart. Then he paused, obviously with an effort, and contented himself with his verbal fury.

"Janice, I just don't understand you! I thought we had an understanding, you and I. And then you run off, disappear without a word or a trace. Do you realize"—his voice became harsh—"the only news I've had of you for nearly three months is copies of bills for merchandise bought on my charge accounts!"

She was aghast. "What? But, oh, no! I wouldn't . . ." She stopped, fearing she had already given herself away. "I—I'll pay for it all," she finished lamely.

"You're darn right you will!" A lean brown hand stretched out and clasped her chin, turning her to face him and forcing her to look into his eyes. They were dark now, shadowed and serious. His voice was soft. "You'll pay in full, my love!"

His face was within a few inches of her own, giving

16

her an opportunity to note the strength of his jaw, almost square, with the faintest suggestion of a dimple in his chin. In spite of its present harshness, his mouth was made for smiling, full and wide, with a slight upward curve at the corners, and although the beautiful clear green eyes had curling lashes, there was no hint of femininity in his face. The whole effect was rather of smooth strength with a hint of mystery in the enigmatic mouth.

For the third time since meeting him she disentangled herself from his hold.

"I don't know what you're talking about." She took a deep breath, trying to steady her voice. "I'm sorry about going off without a word, and all that money spent, and no word to you, and, oh, everything, but I'm here now, and I'm afraid that's all the explaining I can do!" It was, of course, as near the truth as Jasmine could manage. She hoped that this man would be satisfied with that, but as she took a quick glance at him from beneath her lowered lashes, she knew it was not enough.

He was gazing at her with undisguised scorn.

He took her glass from her and roughly pulled her to her feet. "That's not enough! I *demand* an explanation. Heaven knows you owe me one! We had a bargain, remember? Or are you going to deny that too?" Jerking her around to face him, he pulled her close. "Do you dare deny it? Do you? Do you?" For one agonizing moment, as she frantically tried to think of an evasive answer, she thought he was going to kiss her, and her knees felt suddenly weak, so that she had to cling to him for support.

As quickly as he had grasped her he pushed her from him. "Damn it, Janice, I'm tired of these games! Life is just one play-acting role after another, isn't it?"

He sighed wearily, and for the first time Jasmine noticed the tired lines around his eyes and the disillusionment therein.

"You're tired," he said flatly. "And so am I. Tomorrow we'll start again."

He led the way up the stairs, ignoring her protests, calmly assuring her that her car would be safe till the storm's fury abated, at which time he would retrieve both it and all her personal belongings.

At the top of the stairs they turned to the right, where a passageway, open on one side except for a waist-high wooden railing, overlooked the large entrance lounge below. Several doors led to rooms on the other side.

Her escort paused before one of the doors, opened it and motioned her inside.

"Your room is still the same one as before—virtually untouched since you left it, incidentally." Indeed the room still showed signs of occupancy, and Jasmine recognized several of Janice's belongings.

The man had entered the room behind her, closing the door after him, and now he crossed over to another door in one of the walls. He locked this door and came back toward her, the key in his hand.

The speculation in the green eyes and his frank look of appraisal as he allowed his gaze to rove over her slight form made the color rush swiftly to her cheeks. She started to step back away from him, but he was too quick for her.

Taking her firmly but gently in his arms, he lifted her face to his. "I don't know what you've been up to, Janice, or what game you're playing now, but let me tell you that now you're back you'll not escape again—*ever!*"

Mesmerized, as if watching some dream in slow motion, she watched his face lower to hers as his lips claimed her own in a hard, demanding kiss that, when he released her, still seemed to keep her under his spell.

He held out the key. "You'd better keep the door to my room locked. Just now, the way I feel, I may not be able to hold out until our wedding night!"

At the door he turned. "Sweet dreams, my bride!"

When he had gone, Jasmine sank down onto the bed, her thoughts in a whirl. What on earth had she got herself into, she wondered in panic. His bride? Was this the bargain he had referred to? Oh, Lord! She would have to clarify the situation.

She moved toward his door, key in hand, ready to confess her deceit. But she stopped. What had he said? Keep the door locked, because he didn't trust himself. She hardly wanted to burst in on him in his bedroom late at night if he was in that sort of mood.

Remembering the fiercely burning green eyes and the unleashed passion—or was it fury?—she had felt as he had held her close, she could quite believe that he wasn't to be trusted, and she was unwilling to try his patience just now. Better wait till morning.

Too tired for further thought, she undressed. She

found a nightdress in one of the bedside drawers, and in spite of the noisy bursts of the fury of the storm still raging relentlessly outside coupled with the storm raging within her, she was soon asleep.

CHAPTER TWO

Jasmine awoke the next day to sunlight streaming through the windows of her room and a strange eerie silence outside. It took her bewildered senses a moment to readjust to her new surroundings and to realize where she was. When she remembered, she lay for a moment examining the room she had scarcely noticed the previous night.

The head of the bed was placed against the outside wall of the house, with a window on either side. The large picture windows extended almost the whole height of the room and were framed by crushed pink velvet curtains now open to allow in the bright stream of sunlight. Patterned shadows of the trees outside danced on the mauve carpet of the bedroom. The dressing table and wardrobe were undoubtedly antiques and of quite considerable value, judging by the shining well-cared-for condition of the mahogany. There was also a rosewood escritoire along the wall to the right, and in between two doors on her left (she knew where one of them led!) was a fireplace flanked by two armchairs with a small table in the middle. The walls of the room were covered in a pale pink linen embossed with deeper pink stripes. It was a beautiful room, she decided, noting her own reflection in the large mirror of the dressing table. She saw

21

a creamy-faced girl with hair that fell in a tumble of burnished copper curls, a slight figure that seemed half lost in the large queen-size mahogany bed, which had a flounced crushed velvet coverlet made of the same material as the curtains.

A knock at the door disturbed her reverie and she hastily drew the sheets up to her chin.

The woman who entered was obviously the housekeeper. She was a middle-aged lady of ample but neat figure. Her gray hair was plaited and curled into a knot at the nape of her neck. She cast a reproving glance in Jasmine's direction as she placed the tray she was carrying on the night table beside the bed. She looked kindly enough, thought Jasmine, but there was no disguising the fact that the girl in the bed was not her favorite person.

"So you're back again, miss." There was no welcome in the words.

Her sister certainly had made her mark in this household! For the first time in her life Jasmine found her envy of her sister diminishing.

"I'm not staying long. You see—" Jasmine was eager to cast off her assumed identity, but she realized that she owed her confession and explanation first of all to the man she had met last night.

The housekeeper sniffed and prepared to depart. "When you've finished your breakfast Jason said you were to go down to him in the library. He said not to hurry, he can wait!"

These last words were delivered with a note of censure as though the speaker thought he had been kept waiting quite long enough as it was.

Jasmine watched the disapproving back disappear as the door closed. Good gracious! Janice certainly hadn't been a very popular person around here. Jasmine had almost felt sparks coming from the housekeeper. And Jason—thank heaven she had found out at least part of his name—had been, well, strange last night, to say the least. The more she thought over the events of the previous night (as she munched her breakfast with a gusto that reminded her that she hadn't eaten since her toast and coffee on the plane the previous morning), the more she wondered about Jason's feelings for her twin sister. His welcoming words, "So you've come back at last, Janice!" hadn't sounded exactly filled with joy. What was it then that she had felt vibrating through him last night? Love? Fury? Vengeance?

She sighed as she put down her empty cup and threw back the bedclothes. Maybe he had felt just plain lust. After all, he appeared to be a very virile man, and heaven knew he wouldn't be the first man to feel that way about pretty, provocative Janice.

Remembering the overwhelming magnetism of the man waiting for her downstairs, Jasmine shivered and hastened to dress. Further examination of the room revealed that the second door in the communicating wall led to a bathroom, pink-tiled with mauve fixtures and fittings, where she gratefully had a shower before dressing.

She had to use some of Janice's cosmetics which she found in a drawer, for in her haste to leave the car and find shelter she had left everything, including her handbag, in the vehicle. Heavens, her passport, too! Surely it would be safe enough, though. The little car smothered in snow would probably be as impenetrable as a Chubb safe.

She crossed to the window, expecting to see a snowswept drive and a road in the distance. But the sight that met her wondering gaze quite took her breath away. Her bedroom was obviously at the rear of the house and overlooked a sheer drop down craggy cliffs to jagged rocks below, where the ink-blue waters of a lake lapped gently, so gently that scarcely any motion could be detected. Tattered pine trees clung tenaciously to the cliff face all the way down to the water, and the ferocity of the storm was evidenced by the grotesque mounds of snow clinging in weird formations to the trunks and branches.

The rocks below looked sharp and dangerous, but the blue water was indescribably beautiful, like a smooth, velvet carpet spread before her, stretching several hundred yards to the other side of the lake where there were more spiky pines, cliffs, and clumped snowdrifts. There was a strangely quiet calm as often happens before and after a storm. Far away to her left, below the cliffs, Jasmine could see a little harbor, a cluster of houses, and a couple of church towers.

With reluctance she drew back from the window and left the comfort of her room.

She would, she decided, play it straight right from the start—admit her true identity before Jason had a chance to say or do anything.

As she closed her door behind her, she could see over the wooden railing down into the room below.

It appeared to be empty. The fire had already been lit and it cast flickering shadows across the hearth-rug.

Making her way down the wide staircase, Jasmine wondered where the library was situated. She stood in the lounge and looked around her. The fireplace rising in the center blocked her view of the room and served almost to divide the huge expanse in two. Jasmine walked around the central stonework and saw two doors in the opposite wall. One door was slightly open, revealing a large dining table and several chairs. Possibly the other door led to the library? As she stood hesitating, the door in question opened and Jason appeared.

Jasmine felt her mouth go dry and fear clutch at her heart. How was he going to react to what she had to say? How thankful she was not to be Janice, she told herself, thankful not to be pursued and soon married to this haughty male.

Arrogantly, like a lord addressing his humble servant, he said, "I was just coming to look for you. Why do I find you lurking here in the shadows?"

Jasmine lifted her head and tossed back her hair. Now she would tell him and wipe that smirk off his face. How embarrassed he would be to find that she was not Janice to do his bidding and endure his demanding kisses.

"I have to talk to you," she said, brushing past him and entering the library. It was another impressive room, with shelf-lined walls, large windows, and a hanging crystal chandelier. The carpet was a pure snow white while all the chairs were upholstered in plush claret red velvet.

She was momentarily struck dumb until a voice prompted at her elbow, "Yes?"

She took a deep breath. "I'm sorry I kept you waiting. You see, I didn't know the way to the library!"

He turned her quickly toward him.

"Janice! I warned you! No more playacting! You've been in this room a thousand times."

"But it's true! I'm *not* your precious Janice!" She had his full attention now and the direction of his narrowed glinting green eyes. "Janice is my sister— my twin."

Disbelief began to dawn in Jason's eyes, and Jasmine suddenly felt the need to sit down and rest her quaking legs. This was going to be more difficult than she had imagined.

"We're twins," she stated again. "Identical, as you can no doubt testify in view of the mistake you made yesterday. And you seem to know Janice pretty well, I would say." She couldn't resist adding that although she blushed at her own temerity.

Jason was still staring at her without blinking, and she tried to meet his eyes with assurance. It would help if he didn't seem so self-confident and so sure of her too. As though she had tried her every feminine wile on him and he had seen through them all.

She realized he was speaking.

"And, just supposing you are *not* Janice, what would your name be?"

"Jasmine." She found her mouth dry again as he

came toward her. If there had been a trace of uncertainty in him before, it was gone now. He bent toward her. Once again those steely fingers bruisingly clasped her chin and drew her face around to him.

"You lie!" His fingers curled tighter till she almost cried out. But he released her and pulled himself away in fury. "You've heard it said that liars have to have good memories?" He was pacing the room agitatedly, taking long smooth strides like a panther stalking its prey. "Although you apparently don't have one, I do. I remember the day you told me that the only thing you didn't like about yourself was your name. How you wished that your parents had called you Jasmine. You said you hated your everyday ordinary Janice. You honestly expect me to believe you have changed your identity as well as your name and are now some mythical twin sister?"

He stopped by her chair again and Jasmine shrank away from him, shielding her already sore chin from his grasp.

"Twins are supposed to be extra close to each other. If Janice had had a twin, don't you think she would have mentioned you to me?"

Jasmine had the feeling that she was trapped, but she was certainly going to put up a fight.

"Look, J-Jason!" Her tongue tripped over the unaccustomed name. "I don't even care whether you believe me or not. I'm telling you that I'm Janice's twin. My name is Jasmine. Oh, I *know* how she's always envied me my name—but that's all! Do you hear? *That's all!*"

She didn't care that her voice was trembling. She

felt very panicky and her stomach was churning. He *had* to believe her.

"Look at me!" she cried. "Do I really look like Janice? Do I slink into a room and flutter my lashes and gaze rapturously into your eyes?"

She broke off. What a fool he must think her to let all her misgivings of herself to show like that. She jumped up, ready to flee the room, leave this house, quit the country. But he was at the door before she was, in one swift lithe movement so characteristic of everything he did.

She paused and looked up at him. He was no longer haughtily furious. He seemed relaxed again, ready to listen.

"Let's put it this way," he said. "If you are Janice's twin, and I do agree that it's possible, can you prove it to me in any way?"

"N-no, at least. . . Yes, I can! There's my passport. You can't possibly disbelieve that sort of proof, can you?" Uncertainly she looked up at him again.

He was smiling at her and her heart lurched to see how very handsome he looked, leaning against the door jamb, his mouth curled to reveal beautiful teeth. All the cynicism was gone from his face.

"No, I would say that a passport would be pretty conclusive evidence. Where is this important document?"

All the relief fled from her. "Oh, dear! It's in my car. But I can go and get it!"

He laughed. "My dear girl, have you seen what it's like outside?"

He took her hand and led her over to the window.

"See? That's our drive and beyond it is the road—usually very discernible from this window. Your car is probably in any one of a score of snowbanks."

Jasmine was dismayed by the sight that stretched before her. The window itself was half obliterated by a sweep of driven snow, and all that she could see beyond were strange, smooth heaps and mounds of snow whipped into fantastic shapes like peaks of frothy meringue.

"But how will I prove my identity? How will I reach my car? Will we ever get out of here?"

Jason smiled. "Oh, yes, with patience. It may take a few days, but the snowplows will eventually push their way through."

"But that means I'll be here w-with you all that time and you'll . . ." Her cheeks flamed. She had been thinking about his kiss last night, a kiss not to be refused, and wondering how she would manage to repel him if he tried to embrace her again.

The amusement in his eyes told her that he had discerned her thoughts.

"Hmm. You have a good point. If you are not Janice, then I've certainly no business taking advantage of the situation." He released her hand and took a step away from her. "I shall try to curb my lecherous inclinations until we have the matter settled. How's that?"

"F-fine. Thank you." She would have thanked him further, stumbling out her gratitude like a stuttering schoolgirl, but he appeared to have lost interest in her. He moved over to the desk and picked up some papers which he had no doubt been perusing before he impatiently had come to look for her.

"Feel free to explore the house if you haven't seen it already! The only doors where you're not allowed will be locked. Oh—er—and just don't try to escape." He waved over to the window. "That much snow is deadly, I assure you. Even my unwelcome advances must be preferable to that."

Cheeks burning, she left the library and fled to her room.

The bed had been made and a fire lit in the fireplace. Again she admired the room, cozy, old-fashioned, yet not in a stuffy way. Altogether it had a very feminine appeal. Jasmine looked in the large wardrobe and found a few clothes that she recognized as Janice's. At least she would not have to be without clothes until her suitcases were accessible.

She wandered out of her room, deciding to take Jason's advice and explore the house. The temptation to look into the room next to hers was overwhelming, but she resisted such curiosity and walked to the end of the corridor where the balcony overlooking the hall below ended, and the passageway became enclosed on two sides by walls with doors leading off. She surmised that below on her right would be the dining room and the library which she had seen earlier. Curious to know what was above, she tried the only door on that side of the upstairs corridor.

To her surprise a large, well-lighted room lay beyond the door, a room decorated in pale blue with a baby grand piano at the far end and mirrors all around the walls, so that with reflection upon reflection the room looked immense. With a murmur of pleasure she moved over to the piano and lifted the lid. Music was her great passion and delight. Her fingers wandered lovingly over the keys and the beautiful mellow tone enchanted her musician's ear. She sat down on the stool and dreamily began to play some of her favorite pieces, quietly at first and then with heartfelt abandon till her whole heart and soul were lost in the music. She played Beethoven's Moonlight Sonata and the Pathétique, followed by Grieg's Sonata in E and then her fingers irresistibly moved into Offenbach's "Orpheus in the Underworld." As she played, she imagined Orpheus braving the dark terrors of the Underworld in search of his beloved wife, Eurydice. She felt his love and his longing for his wife, and the joy with which he led her back to his world—only to lose faith at the last moment and take that forbidden glance back which deprived him of her forever. As she played the last haunting refrain, she was Eurydice, forced to return to the darkness below while her beloved Orpheus went back to the world of the living. As she pictured him slowly fading away, her roving fingers ached with feeling and her whole body yearned along with them until she felt a salty tear land on her hand. She became aware both that her eyes were full of tears and she was not alone in the room.

She turned slowly to see Jason standing a few feet away, his face strangely pale. He came to stand beside her and his hand stroked the smooth wood of the piano.

"Thank you. That was beautiful. I once knew ... somebody else ... who played that piece." There was a long silence in the room as she sat there waiting for him to speak again. He seemed lost in sad thoughts, and it was quite a while before he became aware of her presence again and shook off his somber mood.

"It seems that my girl has talents that I was not aware of !"

It was on the tip of Jasmine's tongue to point out that she was not his girl, and that Janice couldn't play a single note on the piano. Furthermore her taste in music ran only to the light and modern and no further, but she decided it would be of little use to protest her point at this moment.

Jason had come to tell her that they were to have lunch served in the dining room below. Together they went down to eat.

Lunch was superbly served by the housekeeper, whose name she soon learned was Mrs. Bunty, a name which suited her ample figure admirably. Jasmine tried to convey her pleasure at the meal before her, telling Mrs. Bunty that meals in England were quite different. Mrs. Bunty served grilled steak on an oval wooden platter, garnished with button mushrooms. On a small plate to the side was a delectable-looking tossed green salad and a piping hot bread roll basted with golden honey.

What she had expected to be an uncomfortably silent meal was in fact a pleasant companionable interlude.

Jason carefully kept the conversation away from

the question of her identity, talking not of her at all, but telling her about his work and the area around Lion's Head.

"You would hardly believe it to look outside now," he said, "but this is beef country. Some of the best beef in Canada is produced here."

"Is that what you are then? A beef farmer?"

"Yes and no. I farm beef, but that's only a small part of my life. I have a ranch farther up the peninsula where the land offers good grazing for cattle. Here, where the house is situated, the land is too rocky and tree-covered to be of any use for grazing."

They ate in silence for a while and Jasmine waited for Jason to tell her about the larger part of his life, but all he said was, "Did you look into any of the other rooms upstairs?"

Jasmine shook her head.

"When you penetrate further, you'll see what I really do for a living."

Jasmine was determined to continue her exploration at the earliest opportunity.

But thoughts of seeing more of the house were driven from Jasmine's mind when Jason called her over to the window after their meal. She had not heard the wind rising again, but now she saw that indeed another storm was brewing. The snow that had lain inert and dormant all morning was being whipped into excited swirls by a playful wind.

"It's not much right now," explained Jason, "but if a little breeze can create that disturbance, just imagine what it will be like when the wind rises in a couple of hours or so."

"Are we really going to have another storm?" she asked anxiously, surveying the puffy clouds that were scudding across skies that had now turned gray.

"More than likely." Then abruptly he added, "I hope you can amuse yourself till supper time. I've work to do." So saying, he strode off.

Jasmine sat down at the window, perfectly happy to watch the scene outside. The wind seemed to be blowing in the opposite direction now. Whereas before, the highest banks of snow had been on the east side of the driveway, she could now detect a shifting to the west. Swirls of the white powdery stuff were picked up by the east wind, twirled madly around as if in a gay polka, and deposited in an entirely different area from where they had come.

From time to time the hazy form of a tree would appear in the white veil only to disappear again as the wind danced another gay jig.

Jasmine thought she would never tire of watching, and when large snowflakes began to fall and and add to the disturbance on the ground, she knew that as Jason had predicted another storm was on its way.

She wandered around downstairs, and in a corner of the lounge she found an pile of old Canadian fashion magazines. Delighted with these, she took them upstairs to her room where she sat on the floor by the fire, pored over each one, and dreamed dreams of being rich enough to buy and wear the elegant creations so colorfully displayed.

It was the noise of the rising storm that eventually drew her back over to the window. She saw that the blue satin sheet no longer lay below. Now the gray waters churned and heaved in violent agony, and breakers hurled themselves on the rocks in a rough splintering of foam. The clouds in the sky had turned to angry gray, tinged with an eerie yellow light.

A rap at the door preceded Jason's entrance. He crossed quickly over to the window to stand by her side.

"You're not frightened, are you? These tempests can be terrifying to someone not used to them." His arm gently encircled her, his hand touching her shoulder.

What would he say if she told him that the feeling inspired by his proximity frightened her much more?

"It's rather awesome," she admitted.

Jason's arm tightened, and glancing at his face, she saw that he, too, felt a sort of thrilled anticipation at the clashing of the elements.

As she dressed for dinner she found her thoughts constantly straying back to Jason. The storm reminded her of him. Just as the weather held a hint of suppressed fury ready to burst forth and unleash all its power, so Jason seemed to be a man of mixed passions—smooth and calm on the outside, but who knew what stormy depths churned beneath that veneer?

Jasmine felt at once oddly attracted and repelled, secure at one moment and fearful the next.

Well, she told herself, *you don't have to worry about him. He's Janice's man, and as soon as the storm clears and you can produce your passport, you'll be out of his thoughts.* But this knowledge gave her no satisfaction.

From Janice's wardrobe she chose a viridian green dress, long and romantic, with a deep, ruffled flounce at the hem and a drawstring peasant-style bodice. The color suited her and accentuated both the peach tint of her skin and the copper of her hair.

As she left her room and closed the door behind her, she glanced down into the lounge. Jason stood in the center by the fireplace, his tawny head thrown back, his gaze upon her. Something in his eyes, frankly appraising and subtly sensuous, made her catch her breath. She looked at him, and for a long moment their eyes held, then she broke out of her trance and turned along the passage and down the stairs.

As she reached the bottom, he came toward her, a drink for her in his hand. The inevitable crème de menthe! She took it reluctantly, wondering how to refuse it without seeming rude. Something of her hesitation must have communicated itself to him.

"What's wrong?"

"I-I'm sorry, Jason. I just can't stand crème de menthe."

"Oh, that's right! I'd forgotten you're not Janice, just Jasmine, her twin. How complicated life is, isn't it?"

Something in his tone made her absolutely certain that the crème de menthe had been a deliberate testing on his part. It saddened her to think that just when she thought a quiet understanding had been reached between them there must still be doubts in his mind about her identity. Suddenly her hand was unsteady and her eyes filled with ridiculous tears.

"Damn!" she whispered softly. "Why did you have to do that?" She fumbled for a handkerchief and found one thrust into her hands.

She didn't want him to see her tears. Why give him the satisfaction of knowing he had hurt her? Anyway, by tomorrow she would be able to rescue her passport and prove to him how he had wronged her.

Jason sat down on the arm of her chair. "I'm sorry. That was a dirty trick." He took the handkerchief away from her and wiped away the traces of tears. "I really deserve a kick in the shins at the very least for that, wouldn't you say? Will it excuse me at all if I tell you I really was beginning to believe your story—so much so that I felt bound to put you through just one final test? After all, nobody likes to be taken for a fool, you know."

She did know. And she didn't doubt that he had been taken for a fool more than once by Janice.

Then her heart leaped to think that he really was beginning to believe her. Her shining eyes fixed on his face.

"I'm glad you believe me. I wouldn't try to cheat you; I'm not like . . ." She had been going to say, not like Janice, but realized in time that it would be unfaithful to her twin. "Oh, I do wish we could get to my car and I could show you my passport."

"And establish your identity, and then what?" He was back at the bar. "What will you have to drink, Jasmine?"

"Have you got any sangria? I don't drink much alcohol."

"Coming up. As I was saying, establish your identity and then?"

"Well, do what I came to Canada for."

"Which is?" He handed her the drink and sat down once more on the arm of her chair.

His closeness was alarming and yet exhilarating. She turned in the chair, curling her legs up underneath her so that she was facing him and only had to look up to talk to him face to face.

"Janice left home six months ago and we received only one card from her, from here in Lion's Head, actually and then nothing more. Thoughtfulness never was Janice's strong point, but such a long silence was unusual even for her."

Jasmine took a long slow drink and looked back up at Jason. "I have to find her. Our parents are quite frantic!" Her anxiety overflowed. "Jason, do you think anything has happened to her?"

"Hardly. Janice knows how to take care of herself."

It seemed strange to hear him speak like that of the woman he loved. Well, he must love her, or why else would he marry her?

After dinner they sat again by the fire while the storm outside shrieked in renewed fury.

Their halting conversation had developed into an animated exchange of details of their lives. All trace of former restraint between them had quite vanished.

How pleasant it was to spend an evening like this, with the drama of the storm outside, a good companion and the warmth of the fire inside.

Jason told her about his lonely childhood. His

mother had died when he was only five years old and his grief-stricken father had lived for ten years after that, but had been too wrapped up in his sorrow to bother with a lonely little boy.

Jasmine could picture him sitting by himself on just such a night as this, longing for companionship and love. She wanted to comfort him now to make up for all he had missed and all he had suffered.

Instead she confided in him, too, telling how she had grown up in the shadow of a more vivacious, more popular twin.

"And yet you're determined to find her? I would have thought you would have been glad to have the field all to yourself. Will you really leave here to search for her as soon as the storm has cleared, Jasmine?"

Suddenly her answer seemed very important, and she considered carefully. "Yes. Yes, I have to. You see, I've always been jealous of her and that's what makes it all the more important to do my very best for her. She may need me now, and I would never forgive myself later if I didn't make every effort to find her. Besides, my parents are so terribly worried about her and I can't let them down."

Jasmine fell asleep that night as soon as her head touched the pillow. But it was not a dreamless sleep that claimed her. She dreamed she had found Janice and she was back home again. Her smugly smiling twin returned home in triumph with a pet panther on a chain. It was a sleek beautiful creature that fixed the full agony of its clear green eyes on Jasmine, and yowled in misery as it tried to break its fetters. The yowling increased till she awoke in a sweat to hear the wailing wind, the walls of the house shuddering under its gale force, and finally a terrifying crash and explosion as something was hurled through her bedroom window.

She shrieked in terror, her screams mingling with the baleful laughter of the wind. As she raced for the door, it burst open and Jason, clad in black silk pajamas, gathered her into his arms and held her firmly, dispelling her fears and quieting her shaking limbs. As the fear subsided, she felt herself begin to tremble with a new kind of fear, and lifting her face from Jason's chest, she recognized the same longing in his eyes as was coursing through her own body.

It was only a moment before he bent his head and his lips claimed hers. It was a kiss such as she'd never felt before—a sweet, gentle longing that seemed to make them one in spirit, a joining of two separate people into one compatible whole, a giving and a taking on either side. Jasmine felt as if she were trembling on the brink of something elusively precious, and when Jason finally released her, she knew that they were both shaken.

Jason's voice was husky as he roughly pulled her against him again. "Jasmine, I didn't mean that to happen."

A rap sounded at the door, and Mrs. Bunty's voice called urgently, "I heard a crash. Is everything all right?" Jason bade her enter.

Only then did they look toward the window. The far end of the room was a disaster. A large pine tree, uprooted by the gale, had crashed through the window. Several panes of glass had been broken, and the curtains had been torn by the spiky branches.

"Did any of the glass hit you?" asked Mrs. Bunty, more concerned about the girl than the state of the room.

"I'm all right. I think the glass all flew in the other direction."

"She's nevertheless probably a little shaken, Mrs. Bunty," put in Jason. "I wonder if you'd make up a bed in my dressing room. Now that this room is uninhabitable, she can have my bedroom."

"I certainly will. But first I'll just run and put on the kettle for a cup of tea for the poor child. It works wonders for shock, dear."

Jason's eyebrows quirked in amusement. "The poor child," he quoted. "My dear Jasmine, I have just been supplied with proof more convincing than even a passport. Do you realize that in four months Mrs. Bunty never had a good word to say about your sister? It appears she has noticed something about you that I missed."

Later on, sitting in Jason's big bed and sipping a welcome cup of hot, sweet tea, Jasmine thought over the strange events of the evening with Jason. She couldn't pinpoint the moment when the tension had gone out of their relationship or when he had finally decided that she truly was Jasmine. Perhaps there hadn't been a particular moment. Maybe it had developed gradually from their interest in each other, their exchange of confidences, and their growing trust in each other.

Whatever the reason, she knew that a bond had been forged between them, tenuous as yet, but nevertheless a bond.

Jason entered from the dressing room on one side of the bedroom.

"I'll need the key in the morning so that I can use the other door for my entrances and exits, and allow you to lock this one for—er—security." He paused. "For tonight you'll just have to trust me." He gazed down at her with a strange, unfathomable look in his eyes. He ruffled a hand through her hair, allowing his hand to linger on her cheek momentarily, and then almost snatching it away.

"Good night." Abruptly he was gone.

Jasmine awoke amid foreign surroundings for the second morning. It took her a moment to reorient herself, and then she recollected the events of the previous evening. A quick glance around showed her that Jason's room was much more masculine in tone than the one she had been given to occupy. Gone were the feminine trimmings and pastel colors. Here there reigned a sobriety that was, however, restful. The walls were paneled in a dark wood reminiscent of another era. The furniture was heavy but less ornate than in her room, and the burnt-orange carpet threw a subdued yet cheerful light on the walls. The ceiling was wood, too, deeply carved with horsemen and medieval figures. There was no central ceiling light fixture. Instead, at regular intervals around the walls were brackets, each holding a stained glass light in various colors. It was a room just as delightful as her own but in a different way.

Jasmine's thoughts turned once again to Jason. Was he still asleep in his dressing room, she wondered, but she certainly did not have the temerity to creep out of her bed and look. Her question was soon answered. A moment later, after a quiet knock on the door, Mrs. Bunty entered bearing a tray with a coffeepot, cream, and sugar. She was friendlier this morning, just as she had been the night before.

"Jason has had to go out," she informed Jasmine. "He said he felt sure that you could amuse yourself for today. We don't expect him back till evening."

"But, has the snow stopped to that extent?" Jasmine asked. "Has he been able to get out and through the snow onto the road?"

"Well, not exactly." Mrs. Bunty smiled. "The snow isn't cleared away at all, and it won't be for today at least, but he has gone out through the bush on the snowmobile to check a few things. He can go through the snow on that without any difficulty."

Although Jasmine was not sure exactly what a snowmobile was, the very name seemed to suggest that it was a vehicle expressly designed for negotiating just these weather conditions. She was oddly dismayed that she would lack Jason's company for the day, but at the same time she felt in need of a brief respite: time to herself to think over the events of the past two days and sort out the whirlpool of emotions she experienced every time Jason came near her.

She drank her coffee, luxuriating for a last few minutes in the warmth of the bedclothes and then quickly jumped out of bed, showered, and dressed, ready for a new day.

She would explore the rest of the house, she decided, starting with the downstairs. She was already familiar with the large entrance lounge, the library, and the dining room, but what, she questioned, lay on the other side of the house? No doubt the kitchens would take up a large part of that area, together with the servants' quarters. Was Mrs. Bunty the only servant, or were there more?

Exploring down a corridor that led from the bottom of the stairs in the opposite direction to the library, she came across several closed doors. Remembering that Jason had told her that all doors that were unlocked were hers to penetrate and explore, she tried the first one. It led into a large kitchen-cum-scullery, very rustic in character. Mrs. Bunty was busily sorting out groceries at the large central table. She looked up at Jasmine's entrance.

"Oh! I'm sorry. I didn't mean to intrude," said Jasmine, hastily taking a step backward, meaning to retreat.

"No, no. It's quite all right, dear, you're very welcome to come in here. I guess you'll be glad of a bit of company during the day, and I'm always pleased to see anybody. It sometimes gets lonely here, you know, all by myself. Particularly in the winter."

"Don't you have any help?" inquired Jasmine.

"Well, yes, I do usually for part of the day. But things all get different during a storm. There are two girls to help me part time, but they don't live in. They walk up here from the village, but when it storms as much as this they either get stuck up here and can't return home or, more often, they get stuck at home down in the village and can't manage to get up here."

"I could easily help, you know," Jasmine offered. "If there's anything I could do to help prepare the meals, peel the vegetables or something, I'd be glad to do it." She sighed. "I feel so useless just wandering around doing nothing except amusing myself."

"Good heavens, dear, you're a guest in the house. No need to feel guilty about taking life easy and amusing yourself. However, if you really need something to do, I was going to get these vegetables ready for a stew. If you want to stay and talk to me, I'll be glad of your willing hands. Later on, if you like, I can show you around the rest of the downstairs. There's really not too much to see, but it's nice to know what rooms there are and where all the doors lead. I myself feel lost in a place until I've seen every nook and cranny." Mrs. Bunty laughed. "But then my husband always tells me I'm just an old busybody, anyway."

So there was a Mr. Bunty. As Jasmine set out to work eagerly, she encouraged Mrs. Bunty to tell her more about her husband, which she did with alacrity. He was Jason's right-hand man and often accompanied him on trips to the ranch up north. This time he had gone to check the cattle alone, and see that everything was in order.

As they sorted, peeled, chopped, and diced the wide variety of vegetables, the companionable silence was broken intermittently by Mrs. Bunty who would supply this or that piece of random information which she felt would put Jasmine more in the picture. She had been with the household some thirty-five years, having arrived shortly before Jason's birth. That meant Jason was about thirty-four years old, thought Jasmine, a little younger than she had supposed. Mrs. Bunty had first come to serve the old master, Jason's father, who was a strict taskmaster, but was kind and courteous toward his servants, considerate about their health and well-being. She remembered Jason's mother, too, though she seemed somewhat unwilling to impart too much information about her, simply that she had been a pretty young thing, completely lost for the most part in her great love of music. She had a wonderful gift for playing the piano, and she indulged in it at every possible moment.

"I heard you playing yesterday, dear," said Mrs. Bunty with a nostalgic smile. "It took me back a few years, it did. The very same song the mistress used to play so long ago, over and over again, with a longing and a yearning in her eyes that used to make the master terribly sad. I can see her now, her head thrown back, her eyes gazing into the distance, and little Jason sitting scribbling at her feet, looking up at her with complete adoration."

They finished their tasks, and after putting the stew on to cook, Mrs. Bunty led the way out of the room, wiping her hands on her apron as she went.

"This part of the house is mostly given over to the servants' quarters. In the days of Mr. Jason's father, there used to be a good deal more entertaining than there is now, so they needed more servants. There is a larger kitchen, too, but there's not much use for it anymore with only young Jason here. Occasionally we do give a party, a dance, or some other sort of celebration, and then we open up the big kitchen and get more help in." Mrs. Bunty opened the next door on the right and they were in a far larger kitchen with gleaming chrome utensils and appliances.

"It's kept clean and ready for any sudden emergencies that may arise. I remember last year about this time a whole party of snowmobilers got caught in a storm that was so bad even they were unable to get through. They were held up for three days! Needless to say, we were able to make them welcome and quite comfortable. Fortunately that was one occasion when the two maids from the village had been stranded up here, too, so I had plenty of help. These doors on the left that you see are mainly staff bedrooms, this one is a bathroom for any guests who do not want to make the long trek upstairs, and the door at the far end leads into a little apartment that Mr. Bunty and I have to ourselves."

There was also a woodshed, a sort of extension to the house, where enough logs were kept to last the longest winter. This last room led out to the back entrance.

They adjourned back to the kitchen where the housekeeper had placed coffee on the stove to await their return.

"I can serve your coffee in the library, dear, or maybe you'd just rather relax by the fire in the lounge."

But Jasmine demurred, saying that if Mrs. Bunty didn't mind, she far rather join her in the kitchen.

Mrs. Bunty was only too delighted.

As they talked, Mrs. Bunty told Jasmine how she had first begun to suspect that she was not Janice at the lunch table on the first day after her arrival. "You didn't act superior like that other one, begging your pardon because I know she is your sister." She was absolutely sure of it when she heard Jasmine playing the piano. "Never heard *her* play or show any feeling for music all the four months she was here."

The day passed quickly after that. The storm didn't return, so Jasmine began to entertain hopes that before long the snowplow would get through and clear the road.

After a light lunch, which she ate at Mrs. Bunty's suggestion sitting by the warmth of the fire in the lounge, with a tray on her knees, Jasmine decided that she would explore the upstairs, mainly to find the room that Jason had mentioned provided the evidence as to his main occupation. Although she entered every room, she found nothing except bedrooms, bathrooms, and a room where all manner of paraphernalia was stored. Deeply disappointed, she went back to the music room where she sat and played one favorite piece after another. She ended the little interlude with music that seemed to fit the mood of the weather—some waltzes by Strauss.

A short while afterward, with the music of the waltz still in her ears, Jasmine whirled around the room in the arms of an imaginary partner, her romantic daydream broken suddenly by the entrance door crashing open. She couldn't help emitting a little shriek at the sight of the huge bulky figure outlined in the doorway against the brightness of the snow outside, before she realized it was only Jason clothed for the weather in some sort of bulky coverall that he informed her was called a snowmobile suit.

"If it were red, you'd make an excellent Santa Claus!" she laughed as he hopped around on one foot, trying to extricate the other from the elasticated leg of the suit.

"Laugh all you like, young lady, for tomorrow you'll be clad in one of these. I've decided to take you out with me to the village before you get a feeling of claustrophobia from being snowbound so long."

CHAPTER THREE

That night Jasmine slept deeply with neither a storm nor unpleasant dreams to disturb her. She was still in Jason's room, but he had moved out of the dressing room into one of the guest rooms, ignoring her protests that she should be the one to move.

The next morning she awoke early, feeling very relaxed and eagerly anticipating the promised outing on the snowmobile.

When she arrived downstairs at nine o'clock, forestalling Mrs. Bunty's usual delivery of breakfast in bed, she found Jason in the dining room already eating his bacon and eggs. He raised a surprised eyebrow when he saw her.

"My, but you're an early bird! That feeling of claustrophobia must have really been getting to you, eh?"

He looked quite amused by the excited anticipation she was evincing, jumping up every few minutes to gaze at the mounds of snow outside, and asking for Jason's prediction on the weather.

"I've never seen so much snow before!" she cried. "Will we really be able to get through all that?"

"The snowmobile will. Come on, Jasmine. Sit down and eat. I refuse to take you on an empty stomach."

He watched her delve into bacon, eggs, and toast with the healthy appetite of a young girl, and murmured his approval.

"It's best to go out fully nourished. Snowmobiles are pretty sturdy things, but they do break down sometimes.

"I thought you said we would be able to get through without difficulty. Now you're trying to tell me that I need a pioneering spirit. Will that machine hold two of us?"

"Quite easily. If you had experience in driving one, I would take two for complete safety, but I certainly wouldn't let you try one today under these conditions."

At her look of inquiry he added, "Yes, this is quite a bit of snow even for us. Oh, we're used to snow, but we don't usually get this much in one fell swoop."

After breakfast they relaxed for a while before the fire, drinking cups of warm coffee.

Jason went out and reappeared a few minutes later carrying two snowmobile suits. His was the dark-blue one that he had worn the previous evening, but hers was a vivid orange color.

"Nice and bright so I'll be able to spot you a mile off in the snow." He grinned as he zippered her into its warm depths. In spite of its bulk and warmth, she found that it was very light and did not hinder her ease of movement in the slightest.

Outside stood a yellow Ski-Doo, its bright paint gleaming in the sun. The air was crisp and fresh, and although it was cold enough for her breath to make

51

smoky puffs, Jasmine found the air invigorating after more than two days indoors.

They donned helmets and tinted goggles, Jason explaining that the helmets were a safety measure required by law, and the goggles were advisable because of the blinding effect of bright sun on snow.

The snow was still banked high, virtually untouched and unmarked, its pristine quality unmarred by either the passage of vehicles or feet.

Jason sat astride the snowmobile and Jasmine climbed on behind him. She had to press herself close behind him and his nearness thrilled her. She was somewhat uneasy about putting her arms around him, and feeling her reluctance, Jason turned around to smile at her.

"You'll fall off unless you hold on to me tight," he warned. "Better forget that maidenly modesty in the interests of safety."

She was glad her helmet and goggles disguised most of her blush.

Similar to a motorbike, the speed and braking mechanisms were located on the handlebars. They set off slowly, negotiating the drifts in the driveway with care, and then, when they reached the wider stretch of the road, Jason opened up the throttle and off they roared. The feeling was exhilarating, and Jasmine could feel the laughter gurgling in her throat.

"Like it?" shouted Jason.

"It's wonderful!" she shouted back, wondering if her words reached him.

It was like a ride through a winter fairyland. The

trees and bushes were covered in snow and stood like prehistoric creatures frozen into immobility by the ice. They passed abandoned cars—her own included —distinguishable only by the mounds they made in the otherwise smooth sweep of snow. There were trees on either side of the road, and Jasmine marveled that none of them had been visible in the storm when she had negotiated her little car up this very road. The track they followed bent and curved; they crested a hill and sailed over the rise, the machine's skis losing connection with the ground for a brief time. The view of the village far below them made Jasmine feel as if they were momentarily suspended in mid-air. Then the spell was broken and they swooped down the hill into the village.

Lion's Head was hardly impressive in size. They entered the main street, passing two churches and a police station as well as a post office before Jason stopped in front of a bank and disappeared inside. Left to herself, Jasmine noted with interest the scene around her.

There were very few people to be seen, although other snowmobiles had left tracks in the snow before them, and one or two residents had begun the laborious task of digging their way out of the snow. In the distance, at the far end of the village, a snowplow, with two huge blades was slicing through the mounds and pushing back what seemed like white mountains in order to make the road passable once more.

Across the street from where she sat was a hardware store with a supply of gifts and interesting-looking ornaments in the window, while she thought she could detect farther down the street a restaurant called the Golden Galleon. A couple of gas stations, several houses on the streets crossing through the main one, and that was about all there was to the village.

She mentioned this to Jason when he returned a few minutes later, and he was quick to point out that in spite of its size, there was quite a lot going on in Lion's Head.

"You shouldn't judge it by its size. There's a Rotary Club and a Legion, various church clubs and societies as well as card parties, quilting parties, and a large variety of public suppers and meetings—particularly in the winter."

They started off again and this time Jason steered their direction toward the lakeside and dock where several small boats and craft had been pulled out of the water and were now standing supported on blocks at the water's edge.

"Why are there no boats in the water?" Jasmine wondered aloud, and Jason explained that as the winter progressed and the weather grew colder, the whole bay and much of the lake would freeze over solid with several inches of ice that would crush and damage any boats left in the water.

Jasmine gazed in amazement at the huge expanse of water before her eyes, not able to believe that such a violent mass could possibly be stilled by the ice.

"Just wait and see," laughed Jason. "By February you'll be able to walk from here to the bottom of our cliffs. Look up there." He pointed up the sheer rocks to a house perched on the very edge of the precipice. "Look carefully and you'll be able to make out the broken window in your bedroom. See, there, over on the right where that crazy pine tree is leaning against the house at a drunken angle."

From this angle Jasmine could get a much better idea of where the house was situated in relation to the village. She must have passed through part of the village before reaching the house, but because of the poor visibility in the storm she had been unaware of it. The village clustered around a bay, and on either side rose steep white craggy cliffs, overgrown in parts with pine trees rooted deeply in the cracks and crevices. The cliff opposite them now stretched in a promontory into the lake, and Jason's house was about one mile away from the village along the promontory. There were other houses, too, but Jason's was the farthest.

"What's beyond your house on the cliffs?" Jasmine asked as she pointed upward.

"Nothing but bush—miles of it. Hold tight and I'll take you up there."

And they were off again, sweeping with the effortless grace of a bird back through the main street, up the hill, climbing the cliffs again past Jason's house and driveway this time, and on toward the farthest stretch of promontory.

It was sheer joy to feel the wind rushing past, Jasmine thought, cooling cheeks that were warm and flushed with exertion and excitement. They wheeled and turned off the main track into the trees and wove in and out among the pines, soaring over uneven ground made smooth by the snow. The harsh purring of the snowmobile was the only sound to break the silence of the blanketed world. An occasional jack rabbit, disturbed by their noise, popped out in front of them and then bobbed away into hiding again. The sunlight streaming through the conifers cast dappled shadows on the snowy ground beneath, adding the depth of blues and grays and mauves to the dazzling whiteness.

Jasmine reveled in every moment of the ride, intoxicated by the landscape that was totally different from anything that she had ever seen back home in England. She could feel the vastness of the country around her, could sense that here was a land that was to a large extent untried, only recently discovered and explored by man. She felt at once insignificant in this vastness and yet an essential part of the great scheme of things—a feeling that paradoxically made her both humble and proud at the same time.

She was aware, too, that the man sitting in front of her was more than a little responsible for her new feeling of aliveness. Had she really known him for only two days? In that short time he seemed to have become a part of her very existence. She did not want to examine why she felt this way, fearful of spoiling the joy or of destroying something precious.

Pressing herself close to him as his strong arms and wrists maneuvered the machine over the rocky territory, she knew him for a strong, rugged outdoorsman. The way his head was flung proudly back made her think of the first great explorers of this country—Cabot, Cartier, and Champlain—who had braved the terrors of the unknown, undaunted by the hostile natives and the dark, brooding resistance of the land.

Here was a man who was tough and forceful—everything he did would have strength and purpose. Jasmine caught herself wondering about the obverse side of his nature—surely everyone had a balance in his makeup. Would he not also be tender in moments of repose? And would that tenderness not be manifested as wholeheartedly and with as much of his whole being as everything else he did seemed to be?

Jasmine shivered. Her thoughts were leading her down a path she didn't wish to pursue. Better not think of such intimacies.

It was time for lunch by the time they returned to the house. Jasmine thought that nothing could equal the morning's wonderful experience, but she was proved wrong.

After lunch, when Jason expressed a desire to show Jasmine his "special room" upstairs, she didn't mention that she had already searched for it without success. As he led the way to his secret domain, it became apparent why she had been unable to discover it earlier.

They entered the music room, Jason first with that smooth long-legged stride that Jasmine admired so much. They crossed to the farthest end, beyond the piano, to where a doorway was scarcely discernible, hidden as it was behind one of the mirrors in the wall.

Jasmine was totally unprepared for the sight that met her eyes. As the door opened, a smell of oil and turpentine assailed her nostrils, and an involuntary gasp escaped her lips as a painting on the opposite wall compelled her attention. It was a large canvas— at least four feet by six feet—and it depicted her own dream so vividly that she could scarcely believe that it was not merely a product of her romantic imagination.

Orpheus was leading his beloved Eurydice out of the Underworld, guiding her from a fearful dark world of wild beasts and hideous monsters into a world of light, beauty, and love. In the painting Orpheus was caught in the act of casting an agonized doubting look back. The face was Jason's, with strong cheekbones, high forehead, and tormented green eyes full of despair and longing. Eurydice wore a flowing diaphanous lilac gown, mistily veiling the curves of her slender body. Her arms were out-stretched yearningly towards Orpheus, vainly trying to clasp him in one last embrace. Eurydice's face was that of her twin sister, Janice. But it was a slightly different Janice. Gone was the sharp petulance and pouting that so often seemed to characterize her expression. Her face was softened, her gray eyes mistily blurred as though by tears.

Jason stood at the door, awaiting her reaction. He almost held his breath as he watched the girl move forward as though impelled by some hidden force. She approached the painting and raised both hands as though to cup Orpheus's face in her hands and smooth away the torment from his eyes. Then she shook herself, as if out of a trance, and turned back toward Jason.

Having watched her reaction, he could not doubt her admiration. He did not need her eyes to confirm this as, blurred with tears, they looked at him now.

"J-Jason. It's wonderful. Th-there just aren't any words adequate . . ."

He was moved to come and put his arm around her and draw her close to his side. "Come and see the others too."

There were many more around the walls depicting a wide variety of scenes and situations. Some were Canadian wild life scenes, some landscapes, some historical or mythical scenes from long ago. But all bore one thing in common. They all held vibrancy and drama. In one a snarling wolf protected her cubs from a hungry fox; in another the waves below the cliffs writhed in fury just as she herself had witnessed them two nights ago. A third showed General Wolfe on the Plains of Abraham urging his men on in battle against the French.

As she examined and wondered over each one, Jasmine felt strangely humbled, recognizing that Jason was a man not only of powerful physical force, but also a man of emotions that were every bit as forceful and varied. It was as though the artist had painted part of himself into each canvas, spilling out love, fury, passion, and tenderness in turn.

"I never dreamed this was how you earned your living," she breathed, still not fully able to comprehend the full extent of his talent. "I thought you were more . . ." She stopped. How did you tell a man that he had unsuspected depths without sounding as if you had previously thought him to be shallow?

But he seemed to know what she wanted to say. "You didn't realize that there was so much more to the hidden man?" He smiled a little ruefully. "There are far greater depths to all of us than we imagine, Jasmine. It takes a colossal tragedy or emotional upheaval to reveal them. Then, when one probes further and deeper, it can be almost a frightening revelation." He seemed sad, his eyes tormented just like those of Orpheus in the canvas. What colossal tragedy, what emotional upheaval had forced revelation on him, Jasmine wondered.

He bent his head toward her as he led her out of the room, leaving the door open so that Orpheus was still fully visible. "Now I want you to reveal part of yourself to me. Play for me. You know what piece I want."

And she did play. Sitting at the baby grand, her eyes fixed on the magnificent canvas in the other room, she played once more Offenbach's Orpheus in the Underworld. She knew that for the rest of her life all her dreams and longings would be tied up in that music. Orpheus, as he watched Eurydice fade away from his sight, would always bear Jason's haunting eyes.

That night Jasmine retired to bed early, feeling both physically tired and emotionally drained after the day's events. But although she was tired, sleep evaded her for a long time. Rising in front of her closed eyes, she saw Jason's painting. What deep unfulfilled longing had compelled him to depict that scene in just such a way? Her thoughts winged back to the first day he had found her playing "Orpheus in the Underworld" on the piano in the music room. What was it that he had said? *"Somebody else I once knew used to play that."* Later Mrs. Bunty had supplied the missing identity. Jasmine, too, could picture the little boy listening to his adored mother hour after hour as he scribbled his drawings at her feet. Maybe these scribblings had been the beginnings of his artistic development. What a traumatic experience it must have been for such a young child to lose the adored center of his existence at such an early age.

Then, too, Jasmine remembered that Janice's face looked out of the painting in the guise of Eurydice. Was Jason pining for her twin? Recalling how he had softened her features and made her ethereally beautiful, possessing a gentleness and an elusive charm that Janice herself had certainly never possessed, Jasmine thought how much he must really love Janice. This sudden knowledge thudded like a knell in her heart, for all at once she knew that she had again fallen into the trap of envying her twin—but this time it was much worse—she had fallen in love with her sister's fiancé.

With the taste of salt on her lips, Jasmine fell into a restless sleep.

When Jasmine went down to breakfast the next morning, she found that Jason had already eaten and gone.

Mrs. Bunty told her that he had gone off on the snowmobile again—this time to dig out her car and rescue her suitcases. The first snowplow had passed during the early hours of the morning and had thus rendered the vehicle accessible.

She mooned about rather listlessly after she had eaten breakfast, with a curiously empty feeling hanging over her. With her belongings was her passport, and as soon as she established her identity beyond any doubt, she would be free to leave. After all, she didn't belong here; she had no claim to Jason, his home or anything else to do with his life. With dismay she realized that, to her, firmly seduced by Jason's charm, there was nothing so important in life as this little area of land where Jason was. Lucky Janice! To be offered the love of such a man.

Jasmine knew that she would not be able to leave this place without an essential part of her being wrenched away and forever left behind. But there was nothing she could do. She determined to make the break as quickly as possible.

When Jason returned with her valises a short while later, she was waiting for him in the lounge with an assumed air of impatience. Summoning a carefree eagerness to her voice, she called out to him, "My cases—at *last!*" The inflection in her voice indicated that she was anxious to get this identity business over with so that she could be on her way.

Was it only her imagination that saw a look of pain cross his face?

He stood at the door, tall and erect, with such a serious expression on his face, the green depths of his eyes hidden by his lowered lids, that she thought something was amiss.

"What's wrong?" she cried. "Was my passport not there?"

His lips smiled, but the warmth did not reach his eyes.

"I think so. Your purse was there, at any rate. I leave you to check the contents."

Still he stood at the door, unmoving, just staring at her with a half-frozen expression on his face. She was forced to move toward him and take the handbag from his hand. Very conscious of the eyes that still fixed their unrelenting gaze on her, she opened her bag and found the necessary and long-awaited document.

"See?" She tried to smile brightly. If only he would take that searching gaze off her. She opened the pages. "Here we have one spinster, Jasmine Fleur Nichols. That's me. Silly names, aren't they?" She was babbling now, trying to dispel that awful feeling of emptiness in the region of her stomach. "Our parents obviously got mixed up—it was Janice who should have had those ridiculously feminine and alluring names." Her voice broke. She turned hastily away and moved over to the fireplace, pretending to check the rest of the contents of her handbag.

"So, what happens now?" His voice so close behind her shoulder made her jump. Her startled gray gaze met his clear green one.

"You're leaving?" he asked.

"What else?" she shrugged, trying to convey that it made little difference to her. But within her her heart was crying out silently in an anguish greater than she had ever felt in all her young years. All she could picture stretching ahead was a bleak future looking back to yesterday.

A hand, firm and gentle, turned her face up to his to once again meet his gaze.

"There is something else you could do."

"What?" Did he, too, hear the tremor in her voice?

"You could marry me."

Her gaze widened, Was this a joke? A cruel jest to make her suffer more?

She searched his face, but there was no merriment in it, only an anguished pain hidden in the depths of his eyes. Then she understood. He loved the absent Janice, the woman he thought would never return, and now he thought he had found a substitute. The expression in her eyes made her legs tremble. If only it were for her.

She took a step back. "What about Janice?" she reminded him.

Taking his cue from her, Jason also moved away, putting almost the full width of the room between them before replying in a burst of scarcely concealed passion.

"Janice left months ago. We had a bargain. She promised to marry me in return for my name, my money, and my—" Was he unable to utter the word *love?* He sighed. "I kept my part of the bargain, but she ran off and hasn't reappeared. Oh, she's safe enough, judging by the way she regularly uses my credit cards. But she obviously has no intention of returning, and certainly none whatsoever of marrying me. Jasmine, marry me! I have the license and everything ready."

Jasmine knew it was foolish to even consider the idea, but she heard her own voice asking, "Ready? When for?"

"The day after tomorrow."

"So soon? Oh, I couldn't." What was she saying? Time made no difference. The whole idea was absolutely out of the question.

Jason strode over to her, quick to press his advantage. "I would be good to you, Jasmine! After all, we do have a rapport, you and I—you must have noticed it too. You with your music and me with my painting. We appreciate each other's creativity. We understand each other, don't we?"

Feeling his arms tighten around her and the warm strength of his body close to hers, Jasmine knew she was lost. What she felt for him was so strong. She didn't want to resist. She yearned for him; she couldn't deny him anything. The unbearable thought of life without him quite settled the matter. Oh, she knew he was seeing her twin in her—a girl he could never have—but maybe there would come a day when he would accept her and love her for herself.

As she raised her eyes to his, he read the answer in them. His head bowed closer and his lips took possession of hers. What started as a kiss to seal an agreement developed into something quite different. Her trembling mouth responded shyly at first and then with a will of its own opened to allow his questing tongue to take possession. She could feel the urgent hardness of his thighs pressed against hers until a fiery sweetness began to course through her body, rendering her legs so weak that she would have fallen without his support.

When he let her go, she wondered if he had noticed her abandoned response to his kiss, and if he had, he did not show it. His face merely looked pale and intent and, fleetingly, she wondered if he was thinking about Janice.

There was much to be settled and arranged in the next two days, which was really just as well, for it left Jasmine with very little time to think and perhaps reconsider her decision.

Jason carried her valises upstairs so that she could unpack all her clothes. Not that she had very many, she thought with dismay. Most of her savings had gone toward her fare to Toronto. True, her parents had offered to pay the fare, but she felt that now nearing retirement they needed all their savings.

Jason entered Jasmine's room while she was trying to shake the creases out of her clothes before hanging them up. He offered the perfect solution.

"I have to go to Toronto to settle some business so you might as well come with me. You can go to Chez Milicent along Bloor Street and choose a whole new wardrobe. No! I insist! You'll have to look your best as my wife and it will be my privilege to clothe you properly."

It seemed that there was to be no end to the surprises in store for her. Now that the plows had been through, the road was wide enough for two-way traffic, and Jason urged her to be ready after lunch to make the trip to Toronto. Mrs. Bunty ironed a cream woolen dress that Jasmine had brought with her, and her coat had already dried out from the treatment it had received during her arrival in the storm. How she wished that she had something nicer to wear for Jason to make him proud to be seen with her. She wished it even more fervently when, after lunch, she went downstairs, ready to go.

Jason was waiting for her in the hall, his soft, ash-colored hair curling slightly over the collar of a burgundy leather coat that had narrow lapels and flared from a semi-fitted waist. His long muscular legs looked neat and trim in a pair of beige cavalry twill slacks, and maroon boots completed the outfit. He looked casual in a superbly tailored way.

A gray Lagonda took them through the village and stopped at a field where a Mooney 201 aircraft stood waiting, its sleek smooth lines gleaming in the winter sunshine. The field had been plowed for take-off.

"It's not exactly Toronto International Airport," smiled Jason, "But I assure you that it's just as safe."

It was the first time she had flown in a small plane and she had to still a moment of nervousness. Jason must have sensed this, for his hand descended on hers to press it reassuringly just before they taxied down the runway, gaining speed and easily becoming airborne.

Jason circled the village of Lion's Head a couple of times, showing her the landmarks. From this height they had a bird's-eye view of the little hamlet nestling into a horseshoe-shaped bay. As they gained altitude, Jasmine could see that the entire Bruce

Peninsula was a series of bays and inlets up the east and west sides. The southern end was joined to the mainland at Wiarton while the northern tip jutted out into Georgian Bay. The water was a dark deep blue while the land, covered mostly by snow, showed only intermittent patches of brown and green. A straight, narrow strip down the center of the peninsula, stretching from north to south, marked the main road connecting the peninsula with the rest of civilization.

It was strange to be flying over the very road she had traveled in her car only a few days before. It looked like a long, straight ribbon and from the air Jasmine could appreciate why it had been so easy for her to follow the right route. In little more than an hour Jason pointed out the lights of Toronto airport nearby. But they were not landing there. Jason said it was much easier to land at Toronto Island Airport and take the ferry and a taxi into town. A journey that had taken Jasmine almost seven hours by car in a storm had been achieved in less than two.

There was no snow in Toronto and the sun shone brightly as they landed. The ferry crossing was very brief, just a short little jump across to the mainland.

This was her first sight of downtown Toronto. The skyline was exceptionally attractive with several skyscrapers of various shapes, sizes, and colors. There was also a large needlelike structure with a flattened globe near the top. This, Jason informed her, was the CN Tower, the tallest free-standing structure in the world. One day, he promised, they would eat in the revolving restaurant near the top.

In no time at all they were in a taxi driving up Bay Street. It did not take long to reach Bay and Bloor, and Jasmine pressed her face to the window so that she would not miss anything of this attractive city. The taxi deposited them outside an ornate gothic-looking house bearing a large sign CHEZ MILICENT. Jason whisked her up to the third floor where an extremely chic woman of about forty came forward to greet them, her face alight with pleasure as she recognized Jason.

"Ah, Jason." There was an attractive inflection in her voice. "Comme c'est joli de te voir. I thought you had forgotten me, yes?" Her voice was husky and low and gave the impression of intimacy. She was a very attractive woman, black-haired with a strong wide streak of silver sweeping across her brow and caught behind her head with the rest into a French knot.

Jason obviously knew her well. He kissed her on both cheeks in European fashion and then turned to bring Jasmine into the conversation.

"Jasmine, meet Madame Milicent. She will outfit you superbly! Mili, this is the woman I'm going to marry so you can feel free to exceed yourself."

This statement caused Milicent to look at Jasmine a second time.

"Mon dieu! So you 'ave been caught at last, Jason!" Then she looked back at Jasmine and studied her critically. "You 'ave chosen well, darling! Do you want an appointment in the beauty salon also?"

Apparently she was to have the whole treatment, so she was whisked away by one of Milicent's employees. Jason called out that he would be leaving, but that he would return to pick her up at six o'clock.

Everything was taken out of Jasmine's hands. She didn't have any decisions to make. She spent the next two hours trying on a medley of dresses, coats, suits, and slacks—in fact every type and every variety of clothing until her head reeled. If she indicated that she liked an item, it was placed on one side, but for the most part her choices were made for her by Madame Milicent, who would declare, *"Mais ça c'est juste pour vous!"* and the item would be added to the ever-increasing pile.

Then it was down to the beauty salon where Jasmine was given a new hairdo and a facial. Giorgio exclaimed in delight over the color of her hair, but declared that it was too long and "untamed." He wanted to cut it so that it would fluff out all over in little curls. Rather reluctant to lose what she considered her greatest asset, she nevertheless consented, thinking that at least this would make her look different from Janice.

The finished effect was curiously attractive, the short curls emphasizing her wide eyes and the elfin quality of her features. She was taken back upstairs where all her clothes had been packed into boxes. Only one outfit remained—the one she was to wear that evening for dinner with Jason. She donned a beautiful evening dress in warm apricot nylon jersey with a wide skirt, long sleeves, and a cowl neckline. The color did wonderful things for her skin and hair. Would Jason be pleased, she wondered, as she surveyed herself in the mirror. She experienced a momentary qualm as her eyes dwelt on the cropped curls. If he wanted just a replica of Janice for a wife, that new hairstyle wasn't going to please him. She put on silver sandals, and a large white mohair stole completed her outfit. Scarcely had she transferred her belongings to a small silver evening bag when Jason was standing before her. He, too, had changed and was now elegantly attired in a black dinner jacket, dark trousers, and a pristine white shirt, with a small bow tie at the throat. His manner held an authority which must have been apparent to all, and Jasmine was conscious that many an envious gaze was being cast in her direction as, guided by Jason's hand under her arm, they made their way outside to a waiting taxi.

"Where are we going?" she asked as he settled her inside, but he only smiled and she gathered he intended it as a surprise.

Jason didn't have much to say as the cab drove them back down Bay Street, but Jasmine was vibrantly aware of him at her side, his eyes turned in her direction. As though propelled by his will, she turned her head to meet his candid gaze, but his expression was unfathomable in the dim interior of the cab. Intermittently, as they passed a brightly lighted window or a neon sign, a shaft of colored light would enter the cab, briefly illuminating parts of his face, but his eyes remained in darkness until she could bear it no longer.

"You're not disappointed, are you?" Mentally she berated herself for so foolishly having her hair cut.

How could she have forgotten that in his eyes her only saving grace was her resemblance to Janice?

His voice when he answered was husky and . . . was that surprise she detected? "My golden girl! You're like a pixie or an elf—half woman and half child with that absurdly delightful tumble of curls, that . . . delectable body." His voice, his eyes caressed her until she felt the warmth stain her cheeks and her thick lashes lowered to hide the expression of delight in her eyes.

They drove down to the waterfront and dined in a restaurant called the Cutty Sark that jutted out over the water and was decorated like the interior of a ship. They talked without restraint and danced. Jasmine felt her best, delighted to be elegant and sophisticated, and secure in the knowledge that Jason's good looks were certainly complemented by her own. They made a strikingly attractive couple, and many eyes were on them admiringly as they dined and danced.

Jason was a smooth and accomplished dancer and Jasmine felt they were as one as their bodies molded together swaying to the romantic music.

It was eleven o'clock before they left the Cutty Sark, and Jasmine was beginning to wonder how they would manage the journey back. But Jason had other plans. They were to spend the night at the Royal York Hotel where he had reserved two rooms.

As she undressed for bed, Jasmine wondered how so much could have been crowded into one single day. Was it only that morning that she had sadly decided that she must leave Jason's house as soon as possible? Since then she had pledged herself to him, flown for the very first time in a light aircraft, acquired a whole new wardrobe, and danced half the night away in Jason's arms.

She stood at the window of her room and looked over the lights of Toronto. The tall skyscrapers surrounding the hotel were in semi-darkness; only some of the lights had been left burning. Far below she could see the streets with occasional lights of cars leaving a white or red trail. This was a strange new world to her; it had already proved far more exciting than her rather humdrum existence in England. This was the beginning of a whole new life.

How would it feel to be Jason's wife, she pondered. To be loved and cherished. He would love and cherish her, wouldn't he? This marriage would not be merely a façade to the outer world, hiding a cold, barren relationship. For a moment doubts assailed her, but then she recalled Jason's words as he had left her at the door of her room just a short while earlier.

He had looked down at her, his face in the shadows of the dimly lit hotel corridor, but she had nevertheless been able to distinguish a tenderness in his expression. Cupping her face in his hands, he had said, "After tomorrow I won't have to kiss you and leave you at the door."

Jasmine slept well that night.

The journey back to Lion's Head was made as quickly and as easily as the one to Toronto. In no time at all they were circling the bay, and soon afterward they landed safely. The Lagonda was there to take them back to the house. Jason piled all of Jasmine's new clothes into the back of the car. Although there were still very high snowbanks on either side of the road, the center was bare, the snow having melted in the sun, aided by the passage of many cars.

Back at the house several changes were apparent. The ceremony the next day was to take place in the Anglican church and the reception afterward was to be at the house, followed by a dance in the music room upstairs.

There was activity and bustle throughout the house. In the large kitchen all sorts of delicacies were being prepared under Mrs. Bunty's competent supervision, while some other people had been brought in to decorate the lounge with flowers and festoons.

Upstairs the music room shone. Several occasional tables had been arranged around the room, and a bar installed at one end.

The window in Jasmine's room had been fixed, and there were now no signs of the damage. The curtains had been replaced by gorgeous satin ones and a new matching bedspread had been added.

Jasmine's boxes of clothes were placed at one end of the room and she decided to unpack them and place them in the large wardrobe. What a lot there were. How lucky she was to suddenly find herself able to dress so superbly. Her eyes caught sight of the magazines she had so longingly dreamed over not too many days before, never suspecting even in her wildest flight of imagination that she would so soon be in possession of a wardrobe every bit as costly and elegant.

As she unpacked, sorted, and hung up the clothes, placing the underwear in the dresser drawers and the accessories where she could find room for them, she came across a box that was different from the rest. This was not a blue box embossed with the silver crest of Chez Milicent but a white box with a purple crest on it, bearing the name of a very famous Canadian designer, Odette Desjardins. Jasmine gasped in surprise. She had heard of Odette Desjardins, a young, talented designer who had taken the international world of fashion by storm just a season ago with her stunning collection of wedding dresses. With trembling fingers she opened the box. Tears stung her eyes as she lifted out a gorgeous creation, shaking away the folds of tissue paper. The wedding dress was fashioned in a combination of satin and lace. The high-necked bodice of lace was narrow and plain with a little mandarin collar and long sleeves. A panel of satin was inserted in the front, beginning at a point between the breasts and ending at the waist. The skirt was satin, gathered onto the waistband and falling to just below the knees. A floating half-train was part of the dress. It began at the sides of the waist and extended around the back. Like the bodice, it was lace and it cascaded down to the floor and fanned out to a train at the back.

There was also a similar box containing a veil—a tight band of satin with two lace rosettes to fit the head closely like earphones and encrusted with white flowers.

The knowledge that Jason had been responsible for all this brought a lump to Jasmine's throat and tears to her eyes, and it was thus that Jason found her, sitting amid a froth of white satin and lace and silently crying.

His consternation was apparent as he took her hands and pulled her into his arms, wiping away her tears and gently asking: "You're not regretting it, are you?"

She trembled in his arms. *Regretting it!* How she longed for his tender hold to tighten and his lips to take possession of hers, but he merely held her close, her head pressed against his heart, so that she could hear its even—if rapid—beating.

After he had gone, she felt slightly angry with herself for not having the feminine knowhow to change that comforting embrace into a clinch of wild passion.

Janice would have known how, she told herself, deliberately twisting a knife into her heart.

CHAPTER FOUR

The day of the wedding dawned with clear blue skies and bright sunlight. Sipping her morning coffee while she was still in bed (a luxury which Mrs. Bunty insisted was every bride's prerogative), Jasmine could feel her heart fluttering in her breast. She found it hard to believe that all this was really happening to her. These events all had the quality of a dream, a pleasant dream from which she never wanted to awaken, for although she realized that she was stepping unprepared into the unknown, she felt that she was making the right decision. All this was meant to be, written down in the annals of destiny since the beginning of time.

It was a sobering yet exciting thought that from this day on she would no longer be a single person. From here on her path would run alongside Jason's, crossing, joining, intertwining. She hoped she would be able to live up to Jason's expectations. What exactly were his expectations? She knew she trusted him implicitly. She felt sure he was an honorable man, of high moral fiber, but she would have to tread gently and carefully until she knew exactly how he felt about her. How far, she wondered, would he be willing to allow her to penetrate the armor of reserve he had obviously erected around his emotions? Only time would tell.

Jasmine had telephoned her parents in England to tell them of her marriage. To say that they were surprised would be an understatement. They were puzzled and hesitant, no doubt wondering if their daughter had taken leave of her senses, but they were mollified to hear that she was marrying a man who had befriended Janice for several months and who had promised to help find their missing daughter.

What would happen when Janice was found? How would her reappearance affect Jason? Jasmine knew that her twin's reappearance would create problems both for herself and for Jason. She had tried to induce Jason to reveal why he wanted to marry *her* and delicately inquired about his feelings for her twin, but he had proved very reticent, deftly avoiding direct answers.

A knock on the door heralded the entrance of a young girl. She was about eighteen years old with dark curly hair of shoulder length tied back behind her head in a ribbon. She smiled in a shy but friendly fashion.

"I'm Linda. I help Mrs. Bunty with the housekeeping. I thought you would like some help this morning."

Jasmine assured her that she was more than delighted for both help and company. She did not want to be left alone with her thoughts, and the wedding preparations would not be so nervewracking with someone to help her.

As Jasmine showered, Linda laid out the underwear and wedding dress on the bed, exclaiming in delight over its elegance and femininity. She then helped Jasmine to dress, zipping up the tight-fitting wedding gown and arranging the folds of the skirt to her satisfaction.

"Isn't it heavenly!" she breathed in awe as she surveyed Jasmine in her finery. "Mrs. Bunty said it was an Odette Desjardins, and I was just dying to get a glimpse of it! I've heard of her—who hasn't?—but I've never seen one of her creations before."

"No wonder she's so famous if this is a sample of her work," said Jasmine. "I can tell you that I never imagined that I'd be getting married in one of her wedding dresses when I saw her interviewed on British TV last year."

"How did you manage to decide on which of her models to choose?"

"Well," Jasmine smiled, a pink tinge appearing on her cheeks, "I didn't choose it—Jason did. I didn't even know anything about it until I arrived back from Toronto."

"You mean he chose it all by himself?" Linda was wide-eyed. "There's what I call a man! There's not many guys would be so kind and so thoughtful. But that's Jason all over. He really cares."

Jasmine could see that Jason had a staunch ally and admirer in Linda.

Next Linda arranged Jasmine's hair in neat wispy curls while Jasmine applied a minimum amount of makeup, stressing her eyes, outlining them in soft gray pencil, and delicately shading the lids with an iridescent blue eye shadow. The wedding headdress completed the picture, hugging her head and making her eyes seem huge and bright.

It was time to leave. With a pounding in her chest and a dryness in her throat, Jasmine looked at herself for the last time. She really did feel as if she were saying good-bye to the person she had been for twenty years of her life. She felt she would be intrinsically changed from this moment on.

Mrs. Bunty accompanied her to the door where the Lagonda waited outside. Mr. Bunty was to stand in for her father and give her away in his absence.

At the church, holding tightly on to Mr. Bunty's arm, Jasmine experienced a moment of cold panic. Here she was amid strangers with scarcely anyone to call a friend, committing herself to a man about whom she knew very little. She felt she would have turned and fled had not Jason, waiting at the altar, turned his head and fixed on her a gaze of such infinite tenderness and stunned admiration that her faith in this man was reaffirmed.

She knew that she looked her best as she reached him and his hand took hers. They turned together toward the altar.

Hours later it seemed as if she had gone through the events of the day in a semi-conscious state. She was totally unaware of the ceremony and of making her responses in a clear although trembling voice. She saw Jason only through a haze, for suddenly the enormity of the step she was taking hit her. She and Jason were undertaking a contract for life. It was true that in a very short period of time she had fallen in love with him, but it was still basically a stranger she was marrying. And what of his feelings for her? Dared she hope that he too had experienced that suddenly overwhelming need for her that she felt for him? She doubted that, although she could always hope. She could vouchsafe that Jason was a good man and a sensitive one; from this day forth they would share the intimacy of many hours together as man and wife. Inevitably, she supposed, there would be some dissent and friction along with the affection and companionship.

Although she sensed that Jason liked her, she wondered just how much of herself he saw in her and how much he associated her with Janice. After all, wasn't Janice really the one he loved? Would he forever hanker after the other twin? It was a risk she was willing to take, primarily because apparently, Jason was willing to take that risk and she believed in him and trusted that he would not enter into anything lightly without due caution and consideration. All the same, she realized what a gamble it was.

The reception and dinner at the house passed smoothly, and the dance afterward in the music room, with all the village invited, was a sight to behold, with the glittering chandeliers of the room casting dappled shafts of lights around, the ladies in evening dresses and the men in dinner jackets and dark trousers. The whole colorful scene reflected a thousand times in the mirrors around the walls.

When the guests had all departed, Jasmine went to her room to get ready for bed while Jason made one last check of everything before retiring.

A flimsy eau de Nile nightgown lavishly trimmed with lace had been laid out on the bed. Jasmine undressed quickly and donned the frilly, feminine garment, feeling suddenly shy to notice in the mirror her reflection with her feminine curves delicately revealed through the diaphanous material. She was sitting at the dressing table combing her hair when the communicating door to Jason's dressing room opened and her husband entered. She half turned to look at him and he paused on the threshold. He had changed into blue silk pajamas with a darker blue sash and lapels, the neck wide open to reveal the hair on his chest. She was acutely aware of him and of his virility. His ash-colored hair was curling in little damp tendrils over his forehead, evidencing a recent shower. Jasmine's breath caught in her throat at this picture of masculinity; her eyes strayed to the pulse beating in his throat, the strong breadth of his shoulders, and the slim tapering hips and long legs.

Their eyes met and held. Jason's whimsical smile began in his eyes and curled the corners of his mouth. He slowly moved toward her, coming to stand behind her, his hands electrifying her shoulders as they came to rest there and his gaze caught hers in the mirror.

" 'To have and to hold from this day forth,' " he quoted as he skillfully turned her around and pulled her into his arms, his body molding to hers so that she could feel her own trembling matched by his thrusting urgency. Up to this moment she hadn't known whether theirs was to be a real marriage or not, but now she could not doubt that he was going to expect her to be his wife in full measure. Maybe this knowledge showed in her eyes because he added, "You surely didn't doubt that I would claim my husbandly privileges, did you?"

Her quick blush and lowered lashes spoke volumes and he gathered her closer with a laugh, half amused, half triumphant as his head came down and his lips claimed hers, compelling her to respond with every fiber of her being. She wanted to cry out, "Oh, my darling Jason, I love you, I love you!" but although their vows had been taken and the intimacies of their relationship were made clear, still no words of love had been spoken. She hesitated to be the first one to utter them.

With a smothered exclamation Jason swung her easily, effortlessly, into his arms, and strode over to the bed. His questing mouth caressed her lips, her eyes, the fluttering pulse in her throat, and then moved downward to seek the gentle curve of her breasts. Now his hands were pushing aside her nightgown and stroking and coaxing her body until she gasped in mounting passion and clung to him and welcomed him with an abandon she hadn't known she possessed.

Jasmine awoke to a dull cloudy day that once again threatened snow. The wind was already beginning to rise and the sound of the waves as they hurled themselves in fury against the cliffs could clearly be heard from Jasmine's bedroom. She turned her head and realized that Jason had already dressed and gone, the only evidence that he had ever shared her bed being the impression left on the pillow by his head.

She felt different this morning. She had awakened to a new awareness of herself—or was it just that her body had learned the full meaning of womanhood? With this knowledge had come a new mental awareness too. Jason had revealed new depths in her, physical and mental appetites that she had not hitherto suspected in herself, and she trembled at this knowledge. Had it been a shattering experience for Jason too? She doubted it. A man as handsome and virile as he would hardly have lived almost thirty-five years of his life without some physical assays. Besides, he was a consummate lover—her thoughts delighted in the recollection of his gentle and expert handling of what she had feared would be an embarrassing experience for her.

She hoped she had pleased Jason last night, that not only his sexual appetite had been satisfied but also that he had been glad that it was she whom he held in his arms, not Janice. All at once it seemed very important that it should be so. Jasmine wanted to make an impression on him as herself and not as a substitute.

With these thoughts in mind, Jasmine showered and lavishly sprinkled her tingling body with lemon cologne. From her new wardrobe she chose a vivid red skirt, gored and full, and teamed it with a white silk blouse that had wide sleeves caught into narrow bands at the wrist, and a neck that tied into a bow. It was an outfit that suited her slim form to perfection.

As she went downstairs and crossed the lounge, she saw with a puzzled frown that there was a pile of luggage at the foot of the stairs. Approaching the library, she heard the sound of voices, one Jason's and the other softer, lower. Company so soon after their marriage? She hoped not. The thought of sharing Jason just now was unbearable.

Tentatively she opened the door and entered the library. Jason was standing in front of the desk, his hands flat on the top, bearing his weight as he leaned over to talk to his companion, who was seated in a swivel chair. As Jasmine entered, the chair careened around and revealed the form of her twin sister, Janice—taut and angry like a coiled spring. Janice kept herself in check as Jasmine came to a dismayed halt.

That her twin was here the very day after the wedding was a bad omen. Jasmine did not doubt by the look in Janice's eye that she returned to claim her man. And Jason, how did he feel about her reappearance? Jasmine's eyes swiveled around to the man still standing by the desk. His gaze was guarded as his eyes met hers. Although his face was a mask, a twitching muscle in his temple betrayed his stress.

"Well, well," drawled Janice lazily, effortlessly uncoiling her long shapely legs from the base of the chair. "I hear I have to congratulate the happy couple." She leaned over the desk, her hand outstretched to touch Jason's in a familiar, intimately possessive gesture. "Jason, darling, be a sweetheart and let Jas and me have a girl-to-girl talk. I've simply *reams* to ask her!"

Jason made to comply without saying anything. His face had a closed look, as though he held himself in a strong grip lest his emotions boil over. Jasmine felt her heart turn cold. She wanted to cry out to him, to hurl herself into his arms and feel their protective security, but she dared not. She had the strangest feeling as she mutely watched him leave that she was saying good-bye to him, that any closeness they had shared, brief as it was, was all that she would ever have of him. He had been hers for one short day, but now he was Janice's again.

As soon as the door closed behind Jason, Janice's whole manner changed. Gone was the honeyed sweetness. She hurled herself out of the chair and grasped Jasmine by the shoulders.

"You little cheat! Taking my man like this the moment you got a chance!" Her lip curled, "What on earth you hoped to gain I can't imagine. Do you think that a cold, insipid, colorless creature like you could ever hope to hold on to a man like Jason?" Her eyes raked scornfully the length of Jasmine's figure from curly head to black leather pumps. "I bet he got a shock last night when he took *you* to bed. How could he bear to hold a little nervous mouse like you in his arms after he'd known me?"

Now that she came to consider the matter, Jasmine wondered herself how Jason had been able to stand their wedding night. If he had thought to recreate his moments of ecstasy with Janice, how devastated he must have been to discover that the resemblance ended with the physical. Jasmine could never hope to duplicate Janice's vibrancy and passion. Janice was the substance, and she was the shadow.

"W-what are you going to do?" she asked her sister.

Janice sat down and languidly stretched out her silk-clad legs. She was in no hurry to answer, sensing her sister's uneasiness and knowing that she had the advantage. She searched in her handbag for a cigarette and lighter. Not until she had lit a cigarette and thoughtfully inhaled did she deign to reply.

"Darling, I intend to have him back. Not in six months, not after the divorce, but *now. So don't stand in my way!*"

She got up and moved over to the window, dismissing Jasmine from her thoughts. Sensing this, Jasmine turned to leave. As she reached the door, Jan turned from the window and emphasized: "Jasmine! Don't make it hard for him. He's a very honorable man, you know, and he may feel that he owes you something. You don't want to hold him with that, do you?"

That much was true. Jasmine felt like weeping at the mess she and Jason had created. If only she had had the strength to refuse his tempting, persuasive offer. If only Jason had had more faith in Janice. It appeared that he had been totally wrong when he believed that Janice had no intention of marrying him, for here she had returned with that very intention. No, Jasmine would not make it difficult for him. He should have his freedom. She would reject any indebted kindness he wanted to extend to her.

She reached the sanctuary of her bedroom and

stood against the door, her vision blurred. Yesterday life had been so full of promise, but today it was like a burst bubble, an empty shell, a night without stars.

A figure detached itself from the window, and it was then that she remembered that this was not her room exclusively. Not since last night. She brushed away her tears with the back of her hand, and Jason strode over to her and would have taken her in his arms had she not angrily pushed him away. But he was not to be so easily dismissed. With a deft movement he caught her shoulders, turned her around, and held fast her hands, caught in one of his and imprisoned between his chest and her fluttering heart. Her body immediately leaped to respond to him; the angry green glint in his heavily lashed eyes only served to remind her of the night's shared passion, the hardness of his lips in the night, and the way his searching hands had guided her to him. But knowing her vulnerability to his touch, Jasmine struggled to be free.

"You have no right to do this, Jason."

It was the wrong thing to say, like waving a red flag in front of a bull or jiggling a can of nitroglycerine. His steely eyes flashed in anger. "No right? *No right?* My dear, I have a husband's right—or had you forgotten?"

He stood tall and erect, awaiting her reaction. He was as powerfully attractive today as always, dressed casually in a white sweater and navy blue pants. She noticed the way in which his narrowed eyes were shadowed by the amazing length of his lashes, dark lashes with powdery tips.

Jasmine tried to hold herself away from his disturbing nearness.

"Oh, Jason! If only you'd waited and had more faith in Janice. You were wrong all along, weren't you? She *did* come back, and if you'd waited instead of rushing me into marriage—she was only too willing to marry you after all!"

Jason's angry exclamation interrupted her.

"Are you trying to tell me that you feel you sacrificed yourself for me in vain last night?"

"No—*no!*" That wasn't the impression she wanted to create at all. That would just make Jason feel as if he owed her something. "What I did doesn't matter. But now you'll have to wait for a divorce before you can marry Janice."

Jason's voice was dangerously quiet and Jasmine shivered as his hands tightened painfully on her arms. "And who said anything about a divorce?" Unwillingly she gazed into those cold green eyes. "There will be no divorce, is that quite clear?" He moved away, his expression closed and unreadable. "I'm sorry that what happened last night made you feel like a lamb led to the sacrificial slaughter"—a swift fleeting shaft of pain crossed his face—"but nevertheless my wife you are and such you will remain till death do us part." He was smoldering now with scarcely suppressed fury and Jasmine quivered to be on the receiving end of his furious scorn. "Too bad it sounds like a death sentence instead of a promise of life."

The door slammed behind him and she was left alone; alone with her thoughts and all her regrets, trying to digest the fact that Jason would not countenance a divorce. His words burned in her brain. Was his anger directed at her? She suspected that angry at himself he was venting his fury on her. What had he said? That she was the sacrificial lamb? Too true. Sacrificed on the altar of his worship for Janice. No wonder he regarded the mockery of their marriage as a death sentence.

Jasmine wearily lay down on the bed, fully expecting the onslaught of tears, but she remained dry-eyed. All she could think of was the easy camaraderie and intimacy that had developed between Jason and herself during the last week: the snowmobile ride through the bush, their trip to Toronto, the talks late into the night and the rapport of their shared love of music and art—all shattered now. Would they ever recapture those moments?

The rest of the day passed in a strained atmosphere —for Jasmine at least. She did not see Jason alone at all. Janice seemed ever present and in a way Jasmine was glad because it took the onus off her to provide witty and charming conversation. Janice did just that, openly flirting with Jason, touching him with a possessive hand at every possible opportunity, and putting her lovely copper head close to his to create an intimacy that turned a knife in Jasmine's heart.

That night Jason came briefly to their room to collect his pajamas, and not wanting to hear excuses or recriminations, Jasmine feigned sleep. She sensed he stood for a long moment by the bed, looking down at her before finally extinguishing the light and going out through the communicating door to his own room. She would not let her thoughts dwell on that room next door. She tried to fix her mind on other things, but despite her efforts a picture constantly thrust itself before her eyes—a picture of Janice's lovely laughing face close to Jason's.

The next three days passed in much the same way, Jasmine being treated like an outsider. Her husband was pointedly courteous, but cold. He reserved the warmth of his smile and the charm of his attention for Janice. In her turn Janice barely acknowledged her twin, behaving as though she were a part of the decor—and a rather unpleasing part at that.

At first Jasmine bore this treatment with fortitude, behaving as though she were impervious to the strain, but eventually she knew she would break if she remained in their company for long. She took to merely eating her meals with the other two and then disappearing into her bedroom or the music room, and sometimes into the warm welcome of Mrs. Bunty's kitchen. And she doubted very much whether the other two even noticed her absence.

Thank heavens for her music. The long hours she spent at the piano expurgated part of her grief. Playing all her old favorites, her fingers lovingly lingering over the keys. Music did not transport her to another world or take her thoughts off her sadness, but it calmed her and helped her to come to terms with her unhappiness. The melody that came ever readily to her fingers was the theme from "Orpheus in the Underworld."

And what would she have done without Mrs. Bunty? The housekeeper had come upon her one day in her bedroom, sitting in a chair pulled over to the window, watching the waves fruitlessly self-destruct on the rocks below. How like those waves was she herself—doomed to self-destruction, set on a collision course from which there was no escape. For there could be no fruition of her dreams. Her longings were all bound up in one man, and he was as unattainable as the stars themselves.

Mrs. Bunty did not like to see her alone in her despondent state. Although clearly believing it was not her place to comment on what was going on, she did have eyes, and she had formed a strong liking for Jasmine.

"It's not good for you to spend so much time alone just brooding over things you can't mend," she stated firmly. "If you just hang in there, girl, everything will right itself, you mark my words!" Mrs. Bunty busily changed the bed linen as she talked. "And another thing: I know you derive all sorts of pleasure from that piano, but that's not good either—to shut yourself away from the world. You're getting to be just like the old mistress, Jason's mother. And believe me, it can't be doing Jason any good to hear you either. It must turn a knife in his heart every time. This very same thing happened to her too. Funny how history repeats itself in the most unexpected ways."

Although pressed for more information about Jason's mother and history repeating itself, Mrs. Bunty refused to say much more, merely explaining that Jason's father wasn't the man his mother had truly wanted to marry. Someone else had stolen her first love, a love she yearned for all the rest of her life, deeply hurting those around her by her misery.

Jasmine was deeply impressed with what Mrs. Bunty told her. Poor Jason! He had fallen into the same trap as his mother. He would yearn for his first love, Janice, all his life. She didn't want to hurt him all the more, so she took Mrs. Bunty's advice and spent less time in the music room and more time in the kitchen where the housekeeper and the two girls from the village were usually engaged in household tasks.

She decided that if Jason had no time for her, then she would fill every waking moment of the day with other things. She threw herself into community activities, joining the church choir, the 4-H Club, and quilting parties.

Mrs. Bunty introduced her to quilting. It was a craft that had long since been forgotten in England, but it had been preserved in Canada since the days of the early settlers.

Mrs. Bunty loved to talk about her family and all the things they used to do in the olden days. Her father and mother had come over from England in the 1880s when they were both very small children. After marrying they had lived in a log cabin farmhouse on the other side of the peninsula, and it was there that Mrs. Bunty had spent her childhood. Many were the tales she told of life in those days. It was at times pretty grim. In the winter they would be cut off from the rest of the world for weeks on end. Travel was virtually impossible and huge quantities of supplies would have to be shipped in before the first snowfall.

The only means of travel was horse and buggy or, in the winter, horse and sleigh. The houses were very cold—no central heating, naturally, just a huge fire in the kitchen which would have to heat the whole of the downstairs. In the ceilings of the downstairs rooms were cut circular holes about nine inches in diameter. This would allow the rising warm air to penetrate into the bedrooms and dispel some of the icy chill.

All water had to be brought from a well. At times the water in the pump would freeze up and had to be melted before they could use it.

But in spite of the hardship enforced by farming a poor patch of land and the conditions of the climate, life seemed to have been very rich in many ways. The accent on homemaking, the effort and care that went into making life in the bush as pleasant as possible, the games and pastimes that were a family affair, made life more than just bearable. Mrs. Bunty's mother had been a beautiful quilter, making up her own designs, and teaching her two daughters her skill. Mrs. Bunty's sister lived in the village of Lion's Head and in the winter months she and her friends would still get together on cold, dreary evenings and have a quilting party, all working together on the same quilt, chattering, gossiping, exchanging news and ideas. With so many women working on one quilt, it would quickly take shape and rapidly reach completion, making it a pleasant and rewarding experience to see the finished product grow in front of them.

When Jasmine expressed a desire to see a quilt being made, Mrs. Bunty was immediately full of plans. She would get in touch with her sister to find out when the next quilting party was to take place. As it turned out, there was to be one that very evening and Mrs. Bunty's sister was delighted to be able to invite an interested person from the old country to come and visit.

Mrs. Bunty invited Jasmine to her sitting room so that she could see her quilts. She explained that she still did quite a bit of quilting for herself. Her quilts sold very well to the American tourists who came to the area in the summer months. She had two or three that she had done since last summer that she wanted to show Jasmine. They were all the same design, although worked in different colors. The quilts were made up of blocks eighteen inches square, worked separately and then sewn together to form the required size of spread. The design was called Dresden Plate: It consisted of a large flower, like a daisy, with a round center and sixteen petals fanning out and filling most of the block of white cotton. Once the pieces were stitched together, a border was added, either plain or scalloped, white or colored. All of Mrs. Bunty's quilts had a white background, but the designs varied—one in variegated colors, one all in shades of blue, and one fashioned in yellow and orange.

Mrs. Bunty smiled in delight at Jasmine's praise, but told her, "Just wait till you see my sister's!"

After dinner Jasmine excused herself and went upstairs to put on her coat, boots, and fur gloves. She had learned to dress warmly in this country. When she reappeared, Jason looked up in surprise.

"You're not going out?" It was a question rather than a command, she was pleased to note. She knew that Jason could be difficult sometimes and did not always approve of her outside activities.

"I'm going with Mrs. Bunty to visit her sister. They're making a quilt and I want to see how it's done."

"It's a rotten night outside and Mrs. Bunty doesn't drive. I'll take you both down. Mr. Bunty is out doing a job for me."

He wouldn't listen to her protests that a walk wouldn't hurt either of them, and indeed when they got outside and she noted the weather—blowing winds and whipped snow—Jasmine was glad of the offer. Jason made Mrs. Bunty promise to phone him when they were ready to return home.

"I know *you'll* keep your promise!" he told his housekeeper. "I suspect my little wayward wife here would be tempted to show her streak of independence." But the look he gave her and the way his hand caressed her cheek before he drove off robbed his words of any sting.

Several women had already arrived and were busily setting up the quilting frame and getting the materials ready. Mrs. Bunty's sister explained what they were doing.

"We're putting up the quilting frame tonight because we're just about ready to quilt the blocks to the padded backing."

Indeed the blocks had already been prepared and sewn together. The background was, as usual, white, and the central design was a large full-blown poppy. The petals had been cut out of bright scarlet material and had been attached to the background material with a minute hemming stitch. Each poppy had a yellow center on which had been embroidered black stamens in thick embroidery silk. The blocks had been sewn together, four blocks by six, making a spread of about nine feet by six feet, enough to adequately cover a twin bed. The frame was now being used to quilt the top on to the padded backing; it was about waist high and made up out of lengths of wood with holes and pegs for changing the size. The quilt was attached to the frame at the edges and then rolled over to allow easier handling.

"You see," explained Mrs. Marsden as the ladies set to work, "the design has to be emphasized now by small running stitches around all the pieces so that it will puff up and look embossed."

Large basting stitches held the work in place while the women, who had staged themselves at intervals around the quilt, each set to work on a different area.

"Now you can imagine how long it would take one person to do all this work," smiled Mrs. Marsden. "But many hands make light work. We find that we can have one totally completed in two weeks. It's more fun, too, when we work together."

Mrs. Marsden took Jasmine through to the bedroom to show her some of their finished quilts. There were several designs. One had motifs of a little girl in a sunbonnet, another showed little thatched cottages with a pine tree and flowers at the door. One quilt did not have a white background. Mrs. Marsden explained that it was a special order—a quilt for a teen-age daughter's room. The background was dark brown and the motifs were orange musical instruments and signs, a different motif in every square.

There was a small quilt for a baby's crib, white with chocolate-colored golliwogs on it, and another with the letters of the alphabet for a small child's room. Jasmine particularly liked one quilt with a windmill and large slatted sails in each block. Each windmill was in a different color—only the sails were all in yellow.

"Show her the one you've made for your daughter's engagement party!" urged Mrs. Bunty, and Mrs. Marsden smiled, closed the bedroom door, and brought out what was obviously a well-kept secret. Jasmine gasped in incredulous amazement and admiration. It was beautiful, perfect. Again it was mainly white, but the edges were bordered in ruffled wide white lace. Each square contained a red heart pierced by a golden arrow and entwined around both was a cloud of pale blue forget-me-nots.

"It's beautiful, really beautiful," breathed Jasmine. "May I touch it?" she asked, feeling that she just had to run her fingers lovingly over the upraised design. Mrs. Marsden nodded, pleased with her praise. No doubt her daughter was much the same age as Jasmine, and so she could hope that her approval and delight would be every bit as strong as Jasmine's.

The ladies, who had been busily stitching all this time, now paused for a break—a cup of hot tea and some little cakes. Jasmine had already realized that Christmastime—a season quickly approaching—was when all Canadian cooks came into their own, all making their favorite varieties of small cakes and squares. They were always cut or shaped into pieces no bigger than petit fours, and contained a variety of fruits and nuts, jams and icings. Each cake was small enough so that one could eat three or four without effort, and so enjoy a different taste sensation with each mouthful.

The Canadian ladies had a way of making strangers fully welcome. Jasmine enjoyed their kindness and thoughtfulness, and their interesting questions and comments soon drew her out of her shyness. After the break, they insisted that she try her hand at quilting, only stressing that she should try to keep her stitches small. She spent the rest of the evening outlining the petals of one of the poppies, feeling pleased with herself when she realized that her stitches were in no way disgracing the rest of the quilt.

When Jason came to drive them home, Jasmine was full of all she had seen.

"You'd appreciate some of the designs, Jason. They are really colorful and beautifully made. It would be fun to try and design some."

Even as she was speaking, a plan was forming in her mind. Why shouldn't she herself design some motifs? She had been good at graphic art at school and had once won first prize in a contest for designing the school coat of arms. She made up her mind that this was something she would try in the privacy of her own room. If she made a mess, she wouldn't show anybody. If she did well, she would present the designs to Mrs. Bunty for her use and her sister's too. She had seen enough of the women's work to know that they could cope with any design, however complicated it might be.

She put this plan into action the very next day. After breakfast Jason disappeared into his studio, so Jasmine could be pretty sure that he would stay out of the way till lunch time. Janice was still in bed—she scarcely ever got up before noon.

Jasmine returned to her room. She would need a sketching pad, pencils, and eraser, probably some cardboard to make up the cutouts for any design she liked, and a few crayons or paints would help her envisage the colors.

She knew that Jason would be only too willing to supply the items she needed, but this was a secret and she didn't want to arouse his curiosity. He might even guess what she was up to after their conversation last night about quilting designs.

So she dressed in her snowmobile suit and set out for the village. There were two shops where she thought she might find what she was looking for. The first was a small food market which also sold variety goods. Here she was able to purchase drawing pad, pencils, and eraser as well as a small paint box of water colors. In the next store, where there was also a selection of embroidery materials, she purchased scissors, cardboard, and white linen. Just as she was leaving, her eyes alighted on a cellophane packet of material scraps. Just what she needed. Delighted with her purchases, she sped back to the house.

She spent all the rest of the morning doodling, making thumbnail sketches, examining various shapes and designs. Simple, commonplace designs were easy. What she really wanted to achieve was something original, something that would be evocative of this particular area of Canada. As she doodled, her thoughts were on all the new things she had seen since arriving in Canada. Snow! She smiled. Plenty of that. Pine trees, Ski-Doos, breathtaking sunsets in the frosty air.

Engrossed as she was in her new project, she knew that she had better not shut herself off too much in her own room. Jason did not search out her company very much, seemingly thoroughly engrossed in Janice, but all the same he had lately taken to come looking for her when she was absent for too long. What was it? Was he determined to make her suffer by watching them together? She didn't want him to come bursting into her room and see her working on her designs, especially since she had now begun to formulate an even better idea for a bigger design project that she hoped to surprise him with at a later date.

She made sure that she was still seen around the house. Linda, one of the girls who helped Mrs. Bunty in the kitchen, and the one who had helped Jasmine dress for her wedding, was herself soon to be married, and she never tired of regaling Jasmine with news from the village. She and her boyfriend, Pat, seemed to lead a very active life. It was Linda who suggested that Jasmine should while away the tedium of the long winter months by joining the village drama club.

"There's all sorts of jobs you could do. You wouldn't have to act," explained Linda.

Jasmine thought the idea attractive, but now that she had her designs in progress, she didn't know whether she would have the time. "I'll see what Jason has to say about it," she promised Linda.

Shortly afterward she went in search of Jason. As his wife, she really shouldn't have to ask, but in her present position, a wife who was not a wife, she felt more like an employee who was taking time off.

For once Jason was alone in the library. There was no sign of Janice. He looked up as she entered, the welcoming smile on his face quickly subdued, no doubt as he realized that she was the wrong twin. But no matter what he thought of her, as usual the mere sight of him reduced her to a state of longing.

"C-can I speak to you please, J-Jason?"

"Why not?" He seemed to be in an expansive mood. "We seem to spend all too little time together." Whose fault was that? she wondered angrily. "Come and sit over here by the window. I've been going over some accounts and I could do with a break right now." He urged her to sit in the armchair and disconcertingly perched himself on the arm in his favorite position, the length of his thigh brushing against her arm, his arm over the back of the chair encircling her head. She jumped as his arm descended to caress her shoulders, his fingers idly tantalizing the short curls on the nape of her neck.

"You've been avoiding me, Jasmine."

Dear heaven! If he only knew what his close proximity did to her. "I-I've been busy," was her lame excuse, and the exclamation on his lips proved he did not believe that.

"Hmm! Too busy to find time for your husband? I've heard you playing up there in the music room for hours on end, sounding as if your heart were overflowing." His eyes, as she gazed at him mesmerized, were intriguing green depths hinting at hidden pools of passion. "Tell me, Jasmine, isn't all that feeling wasted in music? Couldn't you find a more personal outlet for the expression of your ardor?" His meaning was abundantly clear as his free hand rose to caress her breast and his head came down close to hers.

"No!" Jasmine would not let him use her again. "No. You've no right to use me like this, Jason."

Whatever spark of passion or affection had motivated him was gone in an instant. Jasmine could feel his withdrawal as definitely as one feels the sun's warmth disappear behind a cloud.

"I was very wrong about you, Jasmine. So very wrong. The unfortunate thing is that, although I've been wrong about people before, it never mattered so much as it does this time. Don't you understand what I've been trying to say? If we want a thing enough, we have to fight for it and never be satisfied with second best. Never!"

So that was it. She was second best to him. He had

thought to be able to forget his longing for Janice and had been disappointed. Was it her fault that she lacked her twin's easy grace and cloying charm? Besides, she was only too well aware of her deficiencies, of how far she fell short of her twin's captivating enchantment. Was there any need to belabor the point continually?

"I'm sorry," she responded stiffly. "But it was your fault, too, you know," she couldn't resist adding. Why should she take all the blame? "How was I to know just how much you expected of me?"

"I guess you're right. I made the mistake of thinking you were mature enough to accept certain things, but I was wrong."

What did he mean? Why did she constantly have the feeling that he was expecting her to grasp a hidden importance in his words? Why would he not explain himself clearly? Oh, what a gap in communication there was between them. What maturity did he expect her to have? The maturity to be able to endure a man's insatiable passion for someone else? She wanted to pursue the question further, but Jason seemed to have lost interest in the issue. He had moved over to the desk and was fiddling with some papers with every indication of wanting to be left alone with his accounts.

"I originally came to ask you something," she reminded him, swallowing a lump in her throat that felt as if it would rise up and choke her.

"Yes. What?"

"Could I join a drama club in the village? They

meet tonight and Linda says she'll take me as a new member."

"Hmm." He looked at her for a long moment, no doubt deliberating whether the idea pleased him or not. She felt like a slave girl who had made an outrageous request of her master. "I . . . don't . . . think so," he replied eventually.

She waited for him to continue, expecting some valid reason for his abrupt refusal, but no excuse was forthcoming. She felt mounting anger within her. When she had first come in to ask him, she hadn't really been enamored of the idea herself, but she didn't like his refusal.

"But why not?" she burst out. "Why not? Am I not a free agent? Am I supposed to sit here forever, waiting for you to turn your charms on me, waiting for you to finish dallying with Janice? Am I going to sit here for the rest of my life while you enjoy whatever distraction comes along?"

She was immediately sorry for her outburst.

With an expression of fury, Jason threw down the papers he had been studying, scattering them in every direction. No doubt he would later regret the fact that he had disturbed the neat order of the pile.

"You pick those up. It was your fault," he stated and then, grasping her by the shoulders and pulling her roughly into his arms, he pressed his mouth on hers, forcing out every ounce of her response to him. She clung to him as if drowning, her first unwilling response mounting into a fiery passion that knew no bounds. Her mind kept telling her that this was wrong, that it was foolish to allow false, vain hopes to engulf her like this and persuade her that she meant something to Jason, that he was kissing her, that he was embracing all the things he liked about her. *No! No!* her mind cried. *This is for Janice. I shouldn't be here, I shouldn't be doing this.* With an effort she wrenched herself away from him and stepped back two or three paces. She would have fled to the door had he not caught hold of her. His expression was bemused as they looked at each other in silence. Both labored under quickened breathing, both no doubt puzzled by the immensity of their reaction to each other.

Jasmine couldn't remove her gaze from Jason's. She was held there as if turned to stone, her eyes pinned to his, her awareness of him at fever pitch. She could understand her inevitable expression of passion in his arms—being so totally in love with him—but what was his excuse? Searching his eyes, she wondered if perhaps he didn't find her just a little attractive and desirable. Why else would he be kissing her when Janice was nearby and available?

Then the spell was broken as Jason pulled her over to the desk and pointed to the scattered papers.

"I know you'll agree that you were partly responsible for that mess, so you can pick them up and put them in chronological order."

He seemed to want to prove some power over her. Meekly she complied, fearing that a refusal or a show of spirit would elicit yet another outburst from him —an outburst which her fluttering heart and shaking limbs told her she could not withstand. She picked up the papers obediently, with a pair of trousered legs on the periphery of her vision, and then she straightened up to sort the bills, fully aware of his scrutiny.

Why did she have to be so conscious of him, so affected by his nearness, so bedazzled by his charm? If only life had been different. If only he would love her as he loved Janice. Suddenly, in reaction to his domineering attitude, his vigor, and his fierce embrace, she felt herself engulfed by a wave of despair. To her hot shame, several drops of salty tears splashed onto the bills.

She felt the papers taken from her hands and gently placed on the desk.

"I'm sorry, Jasmine. You really do seem to bring out the brute in me. What can I say? Why are you crying?"

Jasmine could only gulp and hide her face in the comfort of his shoulder.

"Do you so very badly want to join the drama group?"

She shook her head but still kept her face averted.

Seeking to put right any misunderstanding or hurt his abruptness might have inflicted on her, he forced her to look at him. "I'm a selfish brute, Jasmine. You'll have to get used to that. I've lived a lonely life without the company of others and that very lack made me a selfish man, able to satisfy whatever whim without having to consult the desires or needs of others. Frankly, drama takes up a lot of time, even an amateur production in a small village such as this, and I don't want you away from the house at all hours. We're a newly married couple, remember?"

How could she forget? It seemed to her that he was the one who needed reminding of that fact, having vacated their room to spend all his free time with Janice.

"I'm aware of that, Jason, but how about you? You haven't exactly encouraged my company lately."

Jason's enigmatic gaze searched hers, detecting some slight waspiness in her voice, and a smile of satisfaction spread over his face as he chuckled: "My, my. But I believe the lady's jealous."

"Not at all. It's just that . . ."

"Just what? The only possible alternative to jealousy is that you're cold in bed and wish to remedy the fact, hmm?"

Her cheeks burning, she broke away from him.

"What a horrid thing to say!"

The sound of his laughter filled the room.

"My dear child, I'm only teasing you. When are you going to stop taking life so seriously? Now go upstairs and change for dinner. And bear in mind that I don't expect you to dash off the moment the meal is over. It's a wife's duty to remain to entertain her husband. You will not leave until Janice has retired for the night, is that clear?"

"Perfectly clear." At the door she turned. "I want you to know that I can't stand domineering men."

The sound of his laughter rang in her ears as she raced up the stairs.

That evening Jasmine dressed with particular care. If Jason wanted to extend the olive branch of peace, and did in fact make some semblance of caring for her as a wife and valuing her company, she would certainly meet him at least halfway.

Nevertheless she was puzzled by his request that she should stick by his side until Janice had given up all hope of getting him alone, and had retired to bed. It was the first time that he had given any sign of not being completely seduced by Janice's charms. Could it be that he was tiring of her sister's cloying? Jasmine fervently hoped so.

As she donned a speedwell blue dress, the color of which reflected its delicate shadows in her clear eyes, Jasmine found herself thinking with wonderment that she had known Jason only two weeks and yet, with surprise, she realized that she couldn't remember clearly any time in her life without him. It seemed to her that she had been in a state of half awareness until she had met him; he made her vibrant and alive with feelings, longings, and dreams that filled every waking moment of her day and even invaded her dreams by night.

As she turned for one last glance into the mirror before leaving her room, she was well pleased with the reflection that gazed back at her. The blue dress was tight-bodiced with a gathered flowing skirt and a wide belt that nipped in her waist, thus accentuating its incredible smallness and at the same time persuading the eye upward to the full curves of her youthful breasts. The neckline was demurely high. Now that she had become used to her short curls, she found herself liking her new hairstyle more and more. It gave a youthful, carefree appearance that Janice lacked.

Downstairs Jason was already mixing pre-dinner drinks while a gorgeous Janice, resplendent in shimmering purple satin, lounged on the chesterfield, fluttering her lashes and pouting. Jasmine had the distinct feeling that her appearance had interrupted something. As Jason handed a crème de menthe to Janice, she began wheedling, "Really, Jason. I don't see at all why you shouldn't fly me to Toronto to do some Christmas shopping. After all, your time is your own; you don't have to work to a schedule."

Her tone implied that as far as she was concerned Jason's painting was not really a hard job at all—he could pick up his paints at any time of day or night and daub away.

Jason's mouth tightened as he poured Jasmine's sangria and handed it to her.

"Janice, I'm flattered that you seem to think that painting comes so easily to me, but I assure you that you are mistaken. For me it's one of the most time-consuming and draining jobs there is."

"Oh, well, darling, I didn't mean to offend. Don't be so touchy. Of course your little darling paintings must take time."

Jasmine winced, but Jason's expression was inscrutable as he placed another log on the fire. It was impossible to discern how he felt about Janice's statement. The flickering flames threw his face into violent contrasts of light and shadow, accentuating the curve of his mouth, the strength of his chin, and his finely chiseled high cheekbones.

His eyes met Jasmine's as he sat down in his favorite position on the arm of her chair.

"I thought that after dinner we could take a drive through the town to see the Christmas lights. You've never seen them, Jasmine. They'll be on for the first time tonight. Most of the houses are decorated on the outside with lights, illuminated sleighs, and reindeer and sometimes even more imaginative creations."

"I'd love that."

"And what about me? I haven't seen them either," broke in Janice petulantly.

"Of course I meant you, too, Jan. The car will hold us all and will be warmer than snowmobiles. Besides"—he smiled at Jasmine—"I haven't taught this young lady to drive one yet—something I'll have to rectify in the very near future."

The Lagonda was drawn up by the front door when they left the house a couple of hours later.

Jason went first to open the door.

"Inside, both of you. Quickly! I came out to start the engine fifteen minutes ago so it will already be warm inside."

There was room for three in the front seat and Janice slipped ahead of Jasmine, making sure that she would be sitting pressed close to Jason. She whispered venomously before Jason went around the car and joined them in the front: "After all, dear sister, you've already stolen more than your share. Too bad you're not likely to keep him."

If Jason was surprised or displeased that Janice had placed herself next to him, he did not show it, and off they set on the downward path to the village. Jason stopped the car on the top of the hill so that they could look down at the whole stretch of the village. The road ribboned ahead of them, perfectly straight for about two thousand feet, leading directly to the church at the far end. A religious tableau had been erected outside; the illuminated figures of Mary and Joseph with the baby Jesus in the manger were clearly visible from the top of the hill, while farther back on a slope to the rear of the church could be seen smaller figurines of the three kings bringing their gifts.

In fact the whole village was ablaze in colored lights. It seemed as if every house had added something to the festive scene.

The Lagonda moved forward again and Jason turned it smoothly into the main street, driving slowly so that all the various decorations, colored lights, and illuminated figures could be fully appreciated.

"What a lovely display!" breathed Jasmine, the brightness of hundreds of lights dancing reflections in her eyes. "Does everybody put up colored lights?"

"Just about every home. And, of course, this is just a simple village; we haven't really anything to compare with the larger towns that have much more ambitious displays. In those bigger centers a bus tour is arranged every Christmas for the senior citizens so that they can go around the town and see all the lights."

"Oh, come on, Jason," urged Janice. "Let's go to the Open Road and have a drink. These lights are nice, but once you've seen one, you've seen them all. No wonder they take all the old folks to see them— just about their speed!"

But Jason didn't take them for a drink. Maybe he would rather take her sister to the Open Road, whatever that was, Jasmine thought, when they could have a cozy tête-à-tête by themselves.

Janice was slightly displeased by his refusal to comply with her wishes, and later on, when they returned to the house, she was even more annoyed to find that, contrary to her usual habit of retiring early to her room, Jasmine was ensconced in the large armchair by the fire, showing no signs of disappearing and leaving a clear field for her twin. Of Jason there was no sign.

Janice tried to hide her annoyance; she knew only too well that other tactics worked better against Jasmine. After pouring herself a large crème de menthe, she strolled over to the fire and remarked innocently, staring into the flames, "You're being very foolish, Jasmine. You know you'll only get hurt. I can twirl Jason around my little finger. At one word from me, he'll drop you so fast you won't be able to catch your breath."

Jasmine could feel her mouth going dry. How she wished that Jason would make a reappearance. She knew all too well that she was no match for her twin. She could feel the familiar panic rise within her, the sensation that she was impaled like a butterfly on a pin to a collector's board.

Her voice quavered and sounded unconvincing even to her own ears. "You can't bluff me, Janice! After all, he married *me*, didn't he? Anyway, what's the idea of running away like that if you loved him so much?"

"Love!" Janice laughed. "Poor innocent child. Love doesn't enter into this." Janice sat down, placing her drink on the table beside her and searching in her handbag for a cigarette and lighter.

"Let me tell you something. I don't deny that Jason's a fantastically good-looking man—virile, talented, well thought of in the community. I was tempted to accept his proposal at first, in fact I did accept and strung him along for quite a while."

"Trying to grasp all you could get, no doubt!" Jasmine was pink with fury. "Honestly, Jan! Have you no morals? How could you do that to someone who loved you?"

"Easy. A girl has to keep an eye open for the main chance."

"So what made you change your mind?"

"Oh, I'll admit that I made a big mistake there." She stubbed out her cigarette. "I thought he wasn't rich enough. After all, he's only an artist, you know. So I cleared off. But do you know what I found out from the art gallery where his paintings are selling? My dear, one little painting no bigger than a postcard sold for one thousand dollars while I just stood and gaped. So I went further and asked all about the artist, pretending that I was interested and not revealing the fact that I knew him. Apparently he's worth a couple of cool million. Really, Jasmine, I'd have been crazy not to have come back."

Jasmine felt sickened by her sister's grasping love of money. How horrid she was. She didn't deserve the love of a man like Jason. And poor Jason. Jasmine couldn't help remembering the canvas hung in

Jason's studio; how he must love and long for Janice! Did he know what she was? Could he not see through her soft pretty face to the hardness beneath? Apparently not. Wasn't Janice's face on the Orpheus canvas softened and beautified by the love of the artist himself?

Oh, how unfair and cruel life sometimes proved!

"W-well, you're too late," she managed to state. "He married me, n-not you."

"Well, yes. Who would have thought that my dear, sweeter-than-sugar sister would stoop to such a trick. Little Miss Prim isn't so innocent after all, is she?" She went on. "Let me tell you—" Janice heard Jason's returning step and finished hastily in a whisper. "I'll *prove* to you how much he's under my spell. You heard him refuse to take me to Toronto, didn't you? Well, my dear, by tomorrow he'll have changed his mind." She downed the rest of her drink in one gulp and as Jason entered the room, she raised her voice, "Good night. Sweet dreams, Jasmine."

She managed to seductively brush against Jason as she went toward the stairs, whispering something to him which brought a smile to his lips.

Although she had Jason to herself that evening for the first time in a week, Jasmine felt a knell of doom in her heart which prevented her from enjoying herself as she should.

As Jason outlined his plans for the next day, describing how they would, in true Canadian fashion, go out into the bush to choose their Christmas tree, cut it down, and bring it to the house to decorate, she could only half concentrate, so sure was she that

115

Janice would be working on him to take her to Toronto the next day. It was obvious who would win that argument.

Later on as she undressed for bed, Jasmine sadly wondered how on earth she would manage to wrest Jason's affections from Janice. She wasn't even sure she wanted to do that. If Jason honestly could not see through Janice, would he not be better off receiving his heart's desire? Surely, if he never did see through her insincerity, he would be happy with her. Engaged in these unhappy thoughts, she was startled by a noise in the corridor, and going quietly to her door, she soundlessly opened it and gazed down the passageway just in time to see a blue pajama-clad leg disappearing into Janice's doorway.

So! It was certain now that Janice would be getting her way and going to Toronto. She surely knew how to get around a man. Jasmine grew hot with shame and despair. She realized that Jason was mesmerized with Janice, but was Jasmine herself so unpalatable that her husband would seek satisfaction in another's bed in preference to his bride of two weeks? She flung herself down on the bed, her whole body aching with longing. She knew that she was being inconsistent, that only a short while ago she had been telling him to leave her alone, but that realization didn't help her. Salty tears drenched her pillow. *I'm not even a satisfactory temporary substitute,* she told herself, deliberately trying to inflict more pain. What a failure! She lost all sense of time and wept as if her heart would break.

It was thus that Jason found her when he entered

the room he had not shared with her since their wedding night.

With an exclamation of concern—or was it annoyance—he crossed quickly over to the bed and pulled her quickly into his arms. But as soon as she realized what was happening, she fought him like a wildcat, rejecting his consoling arms and springing away from his touch. Ignoring the hurt in his eyes, she turned on him in fury.

"Don't you dare touch me after you've been to Jan! Let her console you; I apparently can't!" Gone were her tears now. She was white with suppressed pain as she faced him across the wide bed.

All signs of tenderness—had there even been any there before, she wondered—had disappeared now. Jason's whole face was gray and shuttered, all expression gone from his eyes.

"You really don't think much of your husband, do you? Am I such a cad that I'd forget my wedding vows so soon, if at all? And anyway, just what were you doing snooping around and spying on me?"

"I wasn't spying." She knew it sounded unconvincing. "I just heard a noise and happened to look out."

"Is that so?" Jason sneered. "Well, too bad you didn't just happen to eavesdrop too. Then you'd have found out just how innocent my visit to your sister's room really was." His lips curled in contempt. "Next time you must do your work better, dear wife." He moved over to the door, paused, and turned back with a parting thrust. "And now, if you'll excuse me, my love, I'll go and take up where I left off with Jan. Obviously there's no welcome for me here!"

When he had gone, tears of frustration and anger at herself and her own stupidity engulfed Jasmine as she realized she might well have driven him into Janice's eagerly awaiting arms.

She lay awake until well into the night. Finally she came to a decision. If she wanted Jason enough, she would fight for him. What had he said? *Never be satisfied with second best!* Of course he had been talking about himself, but it could apply to Jasmine too. She wanted him and only him. Nobody else would do. There would be no such thing as second best for her. She had to have faith in herself. She would have to remind herself constantly that she was the one he had married, and therefore she had a claim on him.

At last she managed to fall into an exhausted sleep.

CHAPTER FIVE

When she awoke and got up the next morning, there was no sign of Jason or Janice, and upon asking Mrs. Bunty, she was told that both her husband and her sister had left for Toronto. So here was the result of her foolishness! She berated herself for playing straight into Janice's hands. One thing was certain: Whether or not Jason was totally mesmerized by Janice made no difference if she was going to play her part as wife so foolishly.

She sought her usual consolation in the music room, but for once music let her down. Even her favorite melodies brought little peace of mind to her tortured soul and she knew that here was something —someone—who meant more to her than anything else in her life.

Returning listlessly to her room, she sat down by the fire and let her thoughts wander. Had Jason really gone back to Janice's room last night? She couldn't blame him if he had. She had seen him entering earlier and had immediately jumped to the worst possible conclusion, condemning him thoughtlessly without even letting him explain. Did she think so little of him? Was her trust in him so slight? Of course not. It was jealousy that made her fevered imagination create the worst in her mind—jealousy and that confounded feeling of inferiority as far as her twin was concerned. It was becoming a disease, this envy of Janice. How foolish of her to let it destroy any trust and affection that might exist between herself and Jason.

She reminded herself of her thoughts the previous night. *If I really love him enough, I'll think he's worth fighting for, even though I am not usually a fighting sort of person.* Instead of cowering under her sister's dominance, all she had to do was be herself, stand her ground, go on with her life as naturally as possible and not give Jason any cause to find her lacking in any way, either as a wife or a friend.

Meantime she had the whole day to get through by herself—her thoughts constantly invaded by the knowledge that Janice and Jason were together in Toronto, enjoying each other's company.

She stared disconsolately out the window. It was a gloriously sunny winter's day, and looking from the warm interior of the house out onto the deep blue water of the lake and the cloudless clear blue sky, it was hard to believe that it was not very warm outside. It was a marvelous day for a snowmobile ride. Too bad Jason hadn't found time to teach her how to ride one. They looked easy to operate—very similar to a motorbike, she suspected.

An idea was developing in her mind, one that, once formed, was difficult to dispel. Why shouldn't she teach herself how to drive the machine? One summer in England, she had ridden a Lambretta scooter on a camping trip of Devon and Cornwall. A snowmobile was the same sort of vehicle, wasn't it?

She hastened downstairs to put her plan into immediate action. The orange snowmobile suit was hanging on the coat rack at the entrance hall. She donned it speedily and was halfway out the door before a sudden thought occurred to her. If Mrs. Bunty went to look for her and found her missing, and the snowmobile too, she would no doubt worry. Jasmine retraced her steps to the kitchen, popping her head around the door to call out an explanation to Mrs. Bunty. But there was no sign of the housekeeper. Only Linda stood in the kitchen busily making pastry, her hands covered in flour and a white smudge on her nose.

"Mrs. Bunty has gone down to the village to visit her sister," she explained in answer to Jasmine's inquiry.

"Well, when she gets back just let her know that I've taken the snowmobile for a ride. I won't be too long."

Linda smiled. "Have a good time!"

The gleaming machine was in its usual place outside the door, sheltered under the overhanging porch of the house. The key was already in position. Jasmine studied the machine for a moment, then turned the key in the ignition. The engine pulsated into life right away. As easy as that! She had expected at least a little difficulty in starting the machine on such a cold day, but obviously luck was on her side.

She wouldn't go far, just a little way through the bush, following the trail marked out on the trees in red paint that Jason had pointed out to her the other day when they had been out together. What a gloriously happy day that had been. Why had they not repeated it? Clearly nothing of that nature had been possible since her twin's arrival. Janice's coming had spoiled a lot of things. If only she had arrived later. Jason and Jasmine might have had a chance to cement their marriage more firmly. Not much hope of doing that now with Janice hovering and clinging all the time. Take today, for instance. Jason had promised that they would go out together looking for a tree to bring home and decorate. And where was he? Gallivanting around Toronto with Janice. Well, *she* would show him. She would find a tree all by herself and leave him out in the cold for a change.

As she took the trail beyond the house that led toward the thickness of trees stretching back to the farthest reaches of the promontory, Jasmine felt exhilarated. The snow was white and crisp and the sky was high and clear. The Ski-Doo was fairly manageable as long as she kept off the icy patches. She veered and whirled, darting in and out of the trees as if in an obstacle race.

There had been no fierce winds in the last day or two and the snow had hardened, forming a crust over the still soft snow beneath. Evidence remained of a previous tempest. The snow clung to the trunks and branches of trees where it had now settled firmly into hard blotches rather than its earlier cloudy veil. The forest looked dappled, the branches of the pines spotted by clusters of hardened snow, and with the added effect of the filtration of the sun through the sparser branches, a bizarre visual effect was created.

Jasmine did not know how long she swooped and

curved along the trail, breathless and bright-eyed as a child on Christmas morning. She should have been more careful of the time, should have been mindful of how far she had strayed from the house. She had not even given a thought to gasoline until the Ski-Doo began to tire and strain, coughing and whirring till finally, with one last splutter, the engine died. In that very instant Jasmine knew what had happened.

How could she have been so careless! She took off the gas cap and dipped a stick down into the tank. It came out dry, just as she had known it would.

Glancing at her watch, she saw that it was already after midday. She was doubly dismayed with herself. It was bad enough running out of gas, but if she had been considerate, she would have been mindful of the time and would have been well on her way back to the house by the time the gas ran out.

Mrs. Bunty always served lunch at noon. By now she would be extremely concerned about Jasmine's failure to return, probably picturing all sorts of tragedies and misfortunes that could have befallen her.

She supposed that the wisest thing to do would be to leave the machine and start walking back the way she had come. Heaven only knew how long that would take her. Mrs. Bunty would be frantic by the time she got back, and as for Jason, his reaction just didn't bear thinking about. With any luck she would be back at the house before he was.

She set off walking as best she could in the deep snow, but her progress was very slow. Following the grooves carved by the snowmobile tracks aided her somewhat. And there were certainly enough tracks to choose from. Too many! This trail was used by many Ski-Doo enthusiasts, that much was obvious, although she hadn't encountered a single one. She couldn't always see the next red marker on the tree ahead of her, and there were so many tracks wheeling and crossing at different angles and disappearing into the bush in all directions that she became totally confused. To add to her problems, the glare of bright sun on white snow hurt her eyes so much that her head began to pound. She shuffled on doggedly, determined to find her way home before Jason discovered how irresponsible and foolhardy she had been. She slipped and slithered, sometimes hitting her knees against hard rocks hidden under the piled snow, often blinded by the sun or her own frustrated tears. She had been engaged in this hopeless struggle for more than an hour. Surely, soon, she would be able to see signs of the house. But what was this ahead of her? Something yellow gleaming in the snow. A skier? Somebody come to look for her? She increased her speed, running and panting, calling out, until quite suddenly the appalling realization hit her. She was back at her abandoned snowmobile! She had come full circle!

Now she was completely frustrated. It was almost three o'clock. She *had* to find her way back to the house before the sun set. It was already beginning to descend toward the horizon. The sun! Of course! She berated her stupidity. The sun was now clearly pointing its course to the west. She knew that all she had to do was keep it in front of her and she would reach the house. She remembered from the map that this promontory jutted out from the peninsula in an easterly direction. Fortified and cheered now, she once again set out, leaving the snowmobile, a lonely little mound amid the snow and trees.

She realized that she had no time to lose. It was easy to follow the steady course of the sun, but in winter that same sun would set behind the horizon by four thirty. An added danger was the fact that the thick growth of trees surrounding her impeded her view of the horizon, and the sun's progress would all too shortly be blocked by the line of trees ahead. She estimated that in an hour at the very most she would no longer be able to ascertain the true position of the sun in the sky.

The going was difficult, for although a direct line toward the sun would carry her most quickly back to the homestead, she lacked the courage to turn completely away from the snowmobile tracks as they wound in tortuous bends, and cut blindly across country on pure virgin snow where hitherto none had ventured. There was a certain measure of comfort in the tracks that she could not deny herself. As it was, she could feel the panic and hysteria rising within her and she tried to quell her misgivings as she saw that the sun was even now dipping behind the tops of the taller trees.

Shortly afterward it had disappeared altogether. Now was no time for panic. If ever she needed to think clearly, she needed to now. She would negate all her progress if she were to lose her direction. She might even turn a complete circle again and find herself struggling back to her abandoned snowmobile. She came to a clearing and sat down on a rock to ponder her predicament. What on earth was she to do? Would it not be better to stay in the clearing and wait for help to come? Surely she couldn't be all that far from the village. Would not Mrs. Bunty have sent out people to look for her? What on earth did they do in this country about people lost in the bush? She supposed it must be an ever-occurring hazard. But no, anyone brought up in this country would surely have sense to take along provisions, matches, and, above all, a compass. She, in her foolishness, had brought nothing.

A low droning caught her attention. Was that—could it be—another snowmobile? *Oh, please, God, let them find me!* As the drone came nearer and increased in volume, she was better able to ascertain its position. It was approaching from behind her, but the noise seemed high up over her head. It was then that she saw it, and her heart almost burst with relief. Jason's plane! He was looking for her. Thank God!

"Oh, Jason! Jason! I'm here!" she called as she sprang into the center of the clearing and waved her orange-clad arms madly. Surely he couldn't fail to see the bright splash of color made by her snowmobile suit against the snow. Admittedly the sky was rapidly darkening and the shadows cast by the trees had merged into the darkening snow, but surely there was still enough light for the contrast of her suit to show up. She jumped and waved and called. The plane circled again and came in quite low this time. When it was directly over the clearing, the wings dipped once, twice, thrice. A signal! He had seen her!

Laughing hysterically and sobbing convulsively in turns, she sank down into the snow.

All she had to do now was wait. It would be sensible not to move. Jason must have pinpointed her position, though how long she would have to wait before he reached her, she didn't know. She prayed it wouldn't be too long, for the stealthy approach of darkness, the sinister silhouettes of trees, the strange silence of the bush punctuated by the intermittent creak of a branch or the soft, ghostly swoosh of snow relinquishing its icy hold on the pines and falling to the ground, filled her with terror.

A gentle wind had begun to stir among the pines, whispering playfully, teasing her, tormenting her imagination until each murmur, each sigh, each movement filled the forest with a thousand monstrous creatures of the night. Jason's approach mingled with all the other noises. She wasn't even aware of that reality or of the sound of her name being called over and over again. She was rigid with fright when he came upon her crouched in the shelter of a large rock, her arms folded in front of her as if to ward off evil.

Jason had been frightened too. On returning from Toronto he had been met by a half-demented housekeeper, worried out of her mind by Jasmine's prolonged absence. A fruitless search had already been made of the bush within a two-mile radius of the house. The light was beginning to give out. If they didn't find Jasmine before nightfall, the crisis would be even worse. Her snowmobile suit would keep her warm, however low the mercury dipped, but if she were hurt, bleeding, or unconscious, who knew what effect the shock of a night alone in the bush would have. He pictured her, a small, huddled bundle, her orange suit mingling with the flames of her hair. Had she fallen over the edge of the cliff? The little fool didn't realize how carefully the trail had to be negotiated near the cliff edge. And there were so many crevasses in the rocks even where the trail seemed smooth and danger free.

Jason had circled the promontory, looking for signs of a snowmobile hanging over the cliff edge. To his utter relief, there were no such signs. Then he mentally divided the whole area into squares and searched carefully each area in turn. It seemed an endless time before he located the abandoned snowmobile. For a moment his heart lifted, but plummeted again when he realized that Jasmine was not with the machine. Where was she? Poor, silly child. She could be almost anywhere. A search of the immediate area in the vicinity of the snowmobile turned up no evidence of Jasmine. At least there had been no accident, he surmised, or she would have been beside the snowmobile.

He swung the plane in ever widening circles round the Ski-Doo. How far would she have ventured? If the crazy little fool had tried to shelter in a cave, he'd never find her.

He was beginning to despair, his circles now taking him over the homestead; she must have swung completely off course or he would have seen her by now. He swerved in a southwesterly direction and came down low just above the trees, trying to pick out anything moving in the dusk. The snow was beginning to blow before he saw her, a tiny blot of orange in a clearing on the south side of the promontory. She waved desperately, and, dipping his wings, he raced back to the airstrip.

When an hour later, calling her name without response, he came across her huddled against a rock, his first reaction was relieved anger. Taking her hands and pulling her roughly to her feet, he spun her to face him.

"You crazy little idiot! What on earth made you go off like that, Jasmine? In this country we have to be responsible for our actions and so avoid endangering others."

He would have continued but he caught sight of her face—a frozen little face staring sightlessly into his. Recognizing the signs of shock and terror, he pulled her into his arms and cradled her like a child, murmuring softly with his mouth kissing her face, her hair, her closed eyes. Slowly the tension left her body and he felt her relax in his arms.

He held her a short distance away from him.

"Are you all right, Jasmine? We should get you back to the house as quickly as possible. Can you hold on to me behind the snowmobile if I drive slowly?"

She nodded, still clinging to him as he led the way to where he had left his machine among the trees. She wasn't frightened now that he was here, but how he would laugh if he only knew what nameless horrors she had imagined before his arrival.

"You were bearing off too far to the south, although you did basically move in a westerly direction," explained Jason as he settled her on the machine, making sure that she was holding fast to the straps. "If you hadn't made that slight miscalculation, you'd have reached the house a couple of miles back. As it was, you skirted it by a few hundred yards."

On reaching the house Jason insisted on carrying her inside, in spite of her remonstrances and assurances that she was really quite better. But he totally ignored her, sweeping her up as if she were no heavier than a snowflake, and passing an anxious-eyed housekeeper on the stairs.

"She's all right, Mrs. Bunty. Just a little frightened and shocked. I guess she won't do this again too soon," he added grimly as he nudged open the door of her room with his shoulder.

Although she had protested to the contrary, Jasmine felt strangely weak and was glad of Jason's strong arms around her. Was it reaction to the shock of her experience or the close proximity and the warmth of his encircling arms that brought on a convulsive trembling as he laid her down on the bed? To her further mortification, tears began to roll down her cheeks and she found that she could not control either her shaking limbs or her salty tears.

One look at her face told Jason all he needed to know. Quickly he unzippered her snowsuit, throwing it to one side as he began to undress her, and calling to Mrs. Bunty to run the bath water.

"Don't be crazy," he checked her protestations. "I *am* your husband, remember!"

How could she forget as she felt his gentle hands speedily remove her clothing and wrap her in a towel before propelling her toward the bathroom. He urged her into the warm water and said, "Just relax there. I'll be back in a moment with a couple of hot water bottles."

Jasmine had meant to be out of the water and dried by the time he returned, but a lethargy was stealing over her. He was back very quickly, lifting her out of the tub, briskly rubbing her skin to a tingling warmth before he deftly slipped her into a nightgown and carried her to the bed.

She wanted to feel the comfort of his closeness forever, and she struggled to stay awake, but her swimming senses clouded, her limbs felt heavy with warmth and contentment, and soon she was asleep.

Sometime in the middle of the night she half awakened and turned in the bed to feel a warm body next to hers. An arm stretched out and she was gathered close before she again fell into an untroubled sleep, a sleep which lasted through the rest of the night and well into the next day.

Upon awakening, she couldn't marshal her thoughts properly. How long had she been asleep? She felt as if she had lain in a dormant state for days.

The bedroom door softly opened and Jason entered. As he approached the bed, his eyes roved slowly over her, noting with approval that the fiery flush in her cheeks had been replaced by a paler, healthier pink, and if her eyes shone now, it was with pleasure and not fever.

"No need to ask if you're feeling better." He sat down on the bed. "I can see you are." His eyes roamed over her, noting the delightful way her unruly curls had ruffled around her face, his eyes traveling down to admire the curve of her breasts under the pink film. Ever modest, Jasmine lifted the sheets around her and her enormous eyes gazed up at him in confusion.

"Am I going to get an explanation?" he asked, refusing to be tempted by the unconscious appeal in her eyes.

"What explanation, Jason?" Her voice quivered, for she knew very well that under his tolerant gaze lurked a steel will that would mercilessly condemn her thoughtless foolishness.

The eyes regarding her hardened. "No coyness, please, Jasmine. You know what I mean. What on earth possessed you to go off like that, so thoughtlessly oblivious to the feelings of others? Or was it"— the steely gaze narrowed and the mouth set in a thinner line, displaying a touch of cruelty that she had not previously observed or suspected—"was it that you were deliberately playing on the feelings of others?"

"I d-don't know what you mean, Jason. Really I don't. I . . ."

"Don't be obtuse my dear. I see it all now. You calculated that if you tore off into the bush and became lost, you would cause me endless anxiety and pay me back for the way I had treated you the night before." He caught her in a cruelly hurting grip. "Admit it."

"No, Jason, no! Let go of me! You're hurting me! And it wasn't like that at all. I knew I deserved your anger the night before and I wasn't mad at you. I had no thought of paying you back for any imagined insult." She rubbed her wrist where his fingers had left a white imprint. "But I was thoughtless, I'm ashamed to say. I knew I could manage the snowmobile and I didn't think you'd mind if I used it. But I enjoyed myself so much that I lost track of time, and then I ran out of gasoline and, well, you can guess the rest."

"But why on earth did you go so far into the bush in the first place? You should have known the potential danger of such a venture."

She hung her head. "I was looking for a Christmas tree. After all," she reminded him gently, "you did say we were going to look for one and . . ."

"And you thought to peeve me just a little by finding one by yourself, right?"

Her silence told him the truth of that conjecture.

A quick glance at him told Jasmine that he was not annoyed with her, simply rather ruefully self-incriminating.

"I did make that promise, didn't I? Well, let's rectify my omission today." He stood up and moved over to the window. "It's a crisp, sunny day outside. Get dressed and come down to lunch. We'll go *together* this time."

When Jason had gone downstairs, Jasmine dressed

quickly and warmly, deciding on a pair of bright blue slacks topped with a cowl-necked white mohair sweater. She felt fully recovered, both physically and mentally, now suspecting that her hold on Jason was perhaps not as tenuous as she had at first thought.

Her inclination was to hurry through lunch as speedily as possible, but Jason, who was waiting for her in the dining room, would have none of that. He insisted on her eating a healthy lunch, admonishing her that gulping her food too fast would only give her indigestion.

She wrinkled her nose at him.

"You sound like an old man!"

He laughed. "And so I am, compared to you."

"Pouf! Fourteen years difference can scarcely be considered a May–December romance."

He turned to look at her searchingly as she applied a liberal amount of butter to her toast.

"I see the lady has done her homework well."

She had the grace to blush. "Mrs. Bunty and I got talking one day and she told me."

When they were ready to go, Jason brought the big Arctic Cat snowmobile to the door. This was a larger machine than the yellow Ski-Doo, and Jason loaded an extra gas tank on the back.

"We'll rescue the Ski-Doo at the same time as choosing a tree. Do you think you'll be able to manage to drive it home?"

"Of course! I'm not a complete idiot, you know. I would have managed all right yesterday if I hadn't run out of gas." Her cheeks were indignantly pink,

134

and she had the feeling that he was secretly enjoying her indignation very much.

The bush looked different. Much of the snow had dropped from the trees in the night and they now stood bare of the brief white finery. They traveled through the bush on much the same route that Jasmine had taken the previous day. They went from one fir tree to another, deciding whether it was too tall, too small, or too wide.

"That one's lopsided," exclaimed Jason, seeing her eyeing a pine about six feet high that was growing under the shadow of a clump of silver birch trees.

"I don't care. Who said a Christmas tree had to be perfect."

Jason shrugged. "Of course it doesn't have to be— but many people wouldn't be satisfied with a less than perfect tree." He watched her, standing with her feet apart and her hands on her hips, her head tipped back to survey the whole length of the tree. Unconsciously she made a picture of grace and beauty. She loved the tree. It couldn't help being not quite perfect, could it? She must have it to deck in finery and colored lights. She would have nothing else.

It was growing dusk and almost time for supper by the time they returned home with the two snowmobiles and the Christmas tree.

That evening Jason brought the tree from outside and set it up in a corner of the big living room. He had dragged out from the garage several boxes of decorations, streamers, and Christmas ornaments which he placed at Jasmine's feet. While he went in search of a stepladder, Jasmine sorted through all the baubles, deciding which ones to use on the tree and which ones to form into garlands and displays around the room.

There were colored balls, tiny figurines, a set of lights shaped like stars, and another set of tubby Santa Claus figures. Some old-fashioned ornaments of gingerbread houses, candy canes, potbellied stoves, and old-fashioned sleighs were added next, with some handcrafted golliwogs, miniature rag dolls, and teddy bears. Lastly, garlands of tinsel in silver and gold were festooned around the tree and looped over the branches.

Jasmine was in her element, plaiting bows of evergreen into wreaths and adding tiny colored balls to the picturesque groupings.

She was flushed and tired, but happy and pleased with her efforts when she surveyed the finished room.

"I think it's beautiful, don't you, Jason?" She turned to him, her eyes shining. He was watching her with a strange look of caution on his face, a look which suggested that he was appraising not her efforts on the tree, but herself. There was mirrored in his face a sort of hesitation that she could not fathom or interpret. Was he perhaps thinking of Janice and wishing she were there with them?

"You must be tired. Why don't you go up to bed?" was all he said and she felt rather rebuffed as he turned away to check that the glowing embers in the fireplace would pose no hazard during the night.

Deflated, she trailed up the stairs after wishing his back a breathless good night. She told herself that she must not be disappointed if Jason did not always react the way she wanted him to. It was enough for the moment that today they had been together and had enjoyed it.

She undressed slowly, enjoyed a shower, and was no sooner in bed than the door quietly opened and Jason entered, bearing two steaming cups of cocoa.

"This is the only way to end such a day as we have had." He smiled. He too had changed into pajamas. As she drank her cocoa, Jasmine felt a strange fluttering begin in her chest. Jason also appeared nervous and on edge.

Their drinks finished, he placed the empty mugs on the table by the fireplace at the other end of the room. Jasmine sat on the bed, mutely watching every move. Their gazes locked together as he crossed back to her and stood looking down at her, an unfathomable expression in his eyes. Then, with a groan that seemed forced from his very depths, he knelt down by the side of the bed and pulled her to him, his lips fiercely claiming hers as he strained her body against his. Fire coursed through her veins, a warmth that longed for the quenching sweetness that only he could give.

But why did he pull away? Why did he settle her back against the pillows and smooth the sheets back over her? She gazed up at him, the pain of rejection in her eyes.

"What's wrong, Jason?"

"You're tired, and I'm a brute. You've had a busy day on top of a harrowing experience, and for a moment I was forgetting about that. Forgive me for yielding to my own selfishness."

137

She glanced quickly and shyly up at him from beneath lowered lashes that fanned out seductively on the smooth curve of her cheek. "I-I'm not tired, Jason."

With another smothered groan, he stretched out beside her. "I didn't mean to do this—but you're so sweet! You tempt me so!"

Long after he had fallen asleep by her side, Jasmine puzzled about his words. Why had he not meant to make love to her? Did she threaten his attachment to Janice? Or was he loath to use her as a substitute but found himself too weak to resist? She didn't know; but she was determined to fight in any way that offered itself. She wanted this man for herself. War was declared!

CHAPTER SIX

The days they spent alone together with Janice away in Toronto doing her Christmas shopping were among the happiest that Jasmine had ever known. It seemed that each new day brought with it some exciting new experience.

The highlight of all was one day when Jason had been outside shoveling snow; he came rushing inside to urge her to quickly dress in her snowsuit and join him outside. There to her enormous delight she saw an old-fashioned sleigh pulled by two horses. The harnesses had bells attached and, as they trotted smoothly along on the new-fallen snow, a harmonious jingle-jangle could be heard.

When the sleigh started off, Mr. Bunty was sitting at the front to manage the horses, and Jasmine and Jason were the sole occupants of the sleigh. However, as they turned into Main Street, people stopped what they were doing and turned to wave or call out a greeting. Several children engaged in a snowball fight forgot their game and raced alongside, until at a quiet encouragement from Jason and a steadying hand they jumped on board and sat on the sleigh, eyes shining, merry lips parted. That seemed to be interpreted as an open invitation to all, and before long the sleigh was packed with laughing children and adults alike.

They circled the village a couple of times and somebody started to sing "Jingle Bells" and everyone joined in with lusty voices breathless in the frosty air.

Shortly before noon it began to snow, slowly at first, then turning to fast-falling giant snowflakes, threatening to obliterate the world around them entirely and leave them—a crowd of slowly whitening people on an isolated moving island.

People began to disperse then, calling out the greetings of the season as they jumped off the sleigh and made their way home.

"This has been a wonderful morning!" breathed Jasmine. "Oh, Jason, I can't tell you how many things—new things, new sights, novel experiences—have been mine since I came here. It all seems a different world. A magic world. Oh, I do hope, I hope—" She broke off sadly.

"What do you hope?"

"I just wish it would all last."

"And won't it?" He watched her and saw the frown of half-mistrusting sadness replace her earlier lighted face of joy.

"No, it won't last." It was a statement that held a positive ring of finality. She raised troubled eyes to his. "Nothing ever does, you see. This is just an isolated moment of time. When the real world reasserts itself, the magic of this moment will be gone forever."

He was shocked. "What a pessimist you are. You must be crazy if you really think that. Nothing—

140

nothing—can ever destroy this moment if you believe in it." His voice lowered. "Jasmine, we make our own magic moments in life and we can never lose them in our memory."

"But it seems so often afterward they are spoiled or we find out that they didn't mean anything at all."

What she really meant but couldn't say was that maybe these days so happily spent with Jason had assumed an importance for her that Jason did not feel. Maybe all this was going so well between her and Jason merely because Janice was not there to distract Jason.

Jason was watching her carefully, noting each flicker of expression on her face, seeing the uncertainty written there.

"Jasmine, you have to believe."

She laughed. With him sitting close beside her like that, his eyes fixed lovingly on her face, she could believe in anything. "Believe in what, Jason?"

It was several moments before he answered. "Believe in yourself."

The days passed quickly and pleasantly. Jason and Jasmine spent many hours together, but sometimes Jason would disappear into his studio and Jasmine would leave him in peace while she worked on her designs. She had already completed several and taken them to Mrs. Bunty to see if they were workable. She had designed a beautiful block of a huge lion's head with a shaggy mane. The trick was going to be fitting the right shapes of material to make the mane full and shaggy without it being too complicated or lumpy. But Jasmine thought that she had mapped out the pieces nicely and resolved that difficulty. Another of her designs was a tall bushy pine bedecked with colored baubles and snow on the branches. Dancing around the tree was a group of children, their laughing faces lifted to gaze at the star on top. It was an ambitious design that required a great deal of skill in engineering all the little pieces so that they fit just right one with the other.

Mrs. Bunty was ecstatic with the designs and could not wait to take them to her sister to show all the quilting ladies.

When she had finished these, Jasmine turned her attention to something else that she had been mulling over in her mind for quite some time. She thought she would like to try her hand at quilting, but not quite the same sort of thing that the ladies were doing. As she had doodled over her designs, the thought had come to her that some of them would make excellent wall hangings. The design could be prepared on a colored background, and quilted in just the same way. Of course there were unlimited possibilities for designs and they could be much more pictorial and complicated than those used for quilts. It would be a sort of quilted appliqué work.

She had asked Mrs. Bunty to buy her some materials in the village so she was well supplied with all the things she would need. She worked frantically during the moments when Jason was in his studio. She was fortunate that he seemed to be rather busy with some paintings that were to be finished for an exhibition he was to have in Toronto shortly after Christmas, so she had quite a bit of time to herself and need not fear that Jason would come and surprise or interrupt her. She worked long hours, happily hugging the secret of her enterprise to herself.

Sometimes Jason came to her at night. She neither knew nor dared to inquire what propelled him into her bed on those occasions. He would come as a man unable to resist, a man tormented. Always between them, as far as Jasmine was concerned, was the image of her twin. Did Jason visit her when his longing got too much for him? He never spoke much. And she wanted him, needed him so much that she was prepared to accept him without question. Besides, she trusted him, didn't she? She clung to that.

Jan returned from Toronto on Christmas Eve. She had brought with her several house guests who came assured of their welcome since they were friends of Jason's too.

Jasmine was upstairs in her room dressing when she heard the commotion of her twin's return. She could hear the sound of Janice's gay laugh, and one or two other female voices combined with the lower, more muted tones of masculine voices, and intermittently, a louder shout of laughter.

She dressed in something special—a lemon yellow dress in polyester crepe with a horseshoe-shaped neckline that plunged to reveal the curves of her slender figure. It had long tight sleeves and the skirt fell to her ankles in soft gathers. The color reflected even brighter lights into her hair.

Jason popped his head around the door.

"We've five visitors," he said, entering the room

and letting his eyes rove over her approvingly. "If you're ready to come down now, I'll take you and introduce you to them all. There's Paul, my agent in Toronto, who regularly springs his company on me just to make sure I'm keeping my nose to the grindstone and supplying him with paintings; Clarissa, his wife, is there too, and I see that she's brought along her brother-in-law. Her sister was killed in a car crash about six months ago. The other couple are friends of mine from college days. Bill is a travel writer, editor of a Toronto monthly magazine, and Étienne is a writer, too, a theater critic to be exact, who, as his name suggests, is French-Canadian. Come on and meet them."

"I'm glad we're having guests for Christmas," she said as they left the room. And she was glad. The laughter and inconsequential chatter of a crowd would take her out of herself, remove from her the self-imposed burden of trying to be witty with Jason and Janice in turn.

Jason chose to misinterpret her remark.

"Dear me! And I thought you'd be disappointed. I felt sure that you'd want me all to yourself for our first Christmas together."

She flashed him a doubtful glance, not quite sure whether he intended wit or sarcasm.

Downstairs the guests had clustered around the fireplace to enjoy the warmth of the crackling logs after their journey through the snow. Recalling her own treacherous journey and her frozen, hysterical state of arrival, Jasmine knew how they must appreciate the glowing logs. They were all enjoying drinks while, upstairs, Mrs. Bunty and the two housemaids were busily adding the finishing touches to the guest rooms required for the unexpected arrivals.

Six faces turned to greet her as she descended the stairs with Jason; her twin sister merely glanced incuriously at her, her lips thinning in scorn as she noted Jasmine's shyly fluttering lashes and modest air. Of the five newcomers, only one dismissed her as a nonentity; Clarisse Shepherd saw her as a pale shadow of her sister—definitely not the twin to be reckoned with. She should have looked more carefully, particularly at the men's reactions. Paul Shepherd's hand stopped midway as he was going to take another gulp of his drink, while his brother-in-law let out a long low whistle. Jason introduced her as his wife—did Jasmine only imagine the tinge of pride in his voice?—and Bill Tatler, a tall, thin man with stooping shoulders, who looked more than his thirty or forty years, looked genuinely pleased to meet her, his brown crinkle-cornered eyes softening as he held her hand in his.

"You've been holding out on us, Jason." He glanced wryly at his friend. "And I can't say that I blame you either."

"Now I know why Jason's work has been progressing rather more slowly than usual," quipped Paul, not to be outdone.

The fifth member of the party also drew Jasmine's attention. Étienne was a small man by Canadian standards, scarcely more than three or four inches taller than she was, but he had that indefinable something that is called charisma. Jasmine could sense it in him, in his eyes, in the way he moved his head and his hands. He didn't have to speak for her to be aware of it. When she was introduced, all he said was a quietly spoken, *"Enchanté, madame!"* before resuming his seat in the corner of the hearthstone from which position she was acutely aware of his brown eyes surveying her.

One by one the guests drifted upstairs to their rooms, leaving Jasmine alone with her husband. Jason sat in his usual place on the arm of her chair. How she liked that habit of his. It made her feel secure, almost a part of him.

"Whose chair arm did you sit on before I came?" she asked suddenly.

He thought for a moment. "You know, I really don't think I sat like this before you came."

It seemed like a giant conquest to her and she blushed as he asked, "Do you mind?"

"Not at all! You have every right to make any proprietary gesture you like!" Why did the words come out wrong? That wasn't really what she meant.

"That's really not my reason, you know!" She found herself breathless at the expression in his eyes. He went on. "Incidentally, talking of proprietary gestures, I should warn you that I shall be back in *our* room until further notice. I've given my room to Paul and Clarisse for the duration of their stay, so I need somewhere to perch my weary head. I hope I won't disturb you when I work late because then I retire *very* late."

Could that be the reason why there were nights

when he did not come to her room at all? Was it consideration for her that made him sleep in his own room? Oh, she did so hope so.

The men returned to the room far in advance of the women. Clarisse managed to complete her toilette a full half hour ahead of Janice. Clarisse was a tall, dark-haired woman of about forty who had obviously been a great beauty in her youth in a statuesque and classical sort of way. Not that she was by any means over the hill now. Her black hair still shone without any trace of gray. She wore it swept back from her face and coiled smoothly at the nape of her neck. Her high cheekbones, slightly acquiline nose, and finely chiseled red lips all contributed to the impression of rather chilly hauteur. Clear cold eyes of palest blue completed the picture.

She wore a flame chiffon sheath dress that laid bare one shoulder and clung to the smooth line of her body from breast to hip and then swirled out into undulating folds from knee to ankle. She cast a rather patronizing glance at Jasmine as she accepted a drink from Jason.

"Jason, darling, you certainly surprised us with this wife of yours. How come you kept her so secret?" Clarisse turned to Jasmine with a smile that was geared to just the right touch of feminine conspiracy. "We thought no female would ever catch him. Your air of—er—youthful innocence must have seduced him." Her tone implied that the youthful innocence she referred to was nothing more than acute gaucherie.

Jasmine continued smiling amicably, but Clarisse

was not to be deterred. "Just how long have you and Jason known each other?"

Jasmine was somewhat nonplussed for a reply, not knowing whether Jason had divulged to anyone the true circumstances of their acquaintance. She glanced quickly at him, and smilingly, suavely, making it sound the most natural thing in the world, he said, "To tell you the truth, Clarisse, it was almost as much of a surprise to me as it was to you." He looked down affectionately at his wife. "We only met two weeks ago; she just swept me off my feet."

Paul laughed. "One look and she had you, eh?"

Janice made her entrance in a swirling sea-green satin kimono embroidered with colorful birds of paradise in purples and blues. It shone and shimmered, catching the light in all the right places, revealing nothing, but suggesting much. Jasmine felt like a daffodil in a field of orchids beside Janice and Clarisse!

During dinner Jasmine preferred to take a back seat, responding pleasantly when addressed, but concentrating more on studying the others around the dining table.

Paul Shepherd was the most flamboyant figure of the group. At least six feet four inches tall, his unruly hair added to his height as it curled all over his head in Afro style. He seemed to be younger than his wife by about ten years and most of the time he looked and acted like an overgrown schoolboy. He talked big all the time, telling tales of deals he had made, people he had impressed. His rather bloodshot eyes and the way he tipped down his liquor convinced

Jasmine that he was a hard-living man. She couldn't help wondering how Jason had met him and why he had chosen him for an agent.

His wife Jasmine classed as a predatory female, very much alive and vibrant, but too self-assertive and verbally involved in the conversation to impress her as a sincere person.

Her brother-in-law was a schoolteacher named Bob Scott. He seemed to be always smiling and expansive, a joke never far from his lips. His rotund face under a thatch of unruly black hair was half smothered by a bushy mustache and beard. His sparkling blue eyes surveyed the world with equanimity and good humor. He looked—Jasmine decided—as if the world had played one almighty joke on him, and he was determined to enjoy it to the fullest. The only indication he gave that he might have had some sadness in his life was when his glance would perchance fall on the third finger of his left hand, circled by a gold wedding band, and then his right hand would involuntarily touch and stroke the band briefly.

I like him, thought Jasmine. *He has learned how to live with himself and to like himself.*

She was seated in between Bill Tatler and Étienne Laroche. Bill Tatler proved the more loquacious of the two, asking her about her home and her family in England, and telling her in turn of his own travels. His latest explorations had taken him along the southern coast of America. In fact he had only just recently returned from New Orleans.

"Is that really the beautiful city people say it is?"

Bill considered this for a moment. "Well, it just depends on what you mean by a beautiful city. To the modernists nothing less than skyscrapers, new buildings in weird and exotic formations, buildings totally without windows, or, conversely, with nothing but windows—that's what they like. But to me, yes, New Orleans is a beautiful city. And don't think that she is without the modern tough, either. But she has character, atmosphere, and, above all, she has history." He smiled at Jasmine. "You'll notice I said she, for New Orleans is definitely a lady. A little dowdy, a lady who has seen better times and is now indisputably struggling to keep up appearances, but a lady still evidencing the beauty and romance of her youth. She seduces me; she charms and enchants me. The garden area, which is the old American quarter, still has many beautiful old houses, many of which have recently been redecorated and renovated and now stand to testify to their original glory. And the old French quarter, Jackson Square, Bourbon Street, with the mixing of all races, the horsedrawn caleches, the black minstrels, the mingling of a thousand different unidentifiable smells, each of which half evokes some hidden memory from youth." He broke off. "I could eulogize all night. Do I bore you?"

"Good heavens, no!" She shook her head emphatically. "I love old cities, too, although I know them mostly just from reading about them. I haven't been able to do much traveling."

"When the weather improves, I'll take you to our old city of Québec," interrupted Jason from the far end of the table. "She should like that, don't you think, Bill?"

"A great idea!" Bill turned to Jasmine enthusiastically. "Québec is the only remaining walled city in North America. You'll love it. And, incidentally, in many ways Québec is very similar to New Orleans. Both are French-speaking. Québec, too, has its share of picturesque old houses and historical atmosphere. You'll even be able to ride in a horse-drawn caleche."

Étienne who, on her other side, had listened in silence to most of the conversation, now added his opinion that Québec, too, could stand up with pride as an entertainment center. But why wait till the weather improved? The most popular time of all for a visit to that ancient city was surely during carnival time in February when the whole city was snowbound; then she would see palaces constructed in ice, bands, concerts, plays—not to mention the Bonhomme Carnival, a huge snowman who presided over all the activities.

After dinner they all adjourned to the lounge where Paul suggested that they should hold a talent show. Each person had to perform some entertainment lasting not longer than ten minutes.

The idea was received enthusiastically, especially by Clarisse and Janice. Everyone scattered to make hasty preparations.

Jasmine wondered what Clarisse would do. She already knew what Janice would do. She would do a modern dance routine, for when Jasmine had shown so much promise as a pianist and Janice had shown none whatsoever, Janice had been given dancing lessons so that she would not feel eclipsed by her twin. Jasmine had to admit that Janice was really rather good.

The chairs and chesterfield were arranged so that everybody could enjoy both the fire and the show.

Janice went first. She had searched out a record of one of the modern dances from *West Side Story.* She had also quickly sped upstairs and—in record time for her—had changed into a black leotard and tights. Her lovely hair gleamed against the shiny nylon outfit; her skin shone in creamy contrast. As she went through the intricate steps and movements, her lovely body was shown to advantage. Not that it was a display of body, Jasmine had to admit; it was rather a display of controlled movement—a poem in motion she had once heard one of Janice's admirers say, and she honestly thought he was right.

Bob's turn was next. He carefully explained that the only talents he felt he possessed were the ones he used daily in the classroom. "Of course, a teacher has to be a bit of a clown sometimes, and that's what I'm going to do in mime." He performed a Red Skelton type of skit, his eyes acquiring a watery expression as he went through the motions of waking up in the morning and making his search through garbage and trash cans looking for an appetizing breakfast. He was a natural comic, entirely credible as he portrayed the pathetic figure.

Clarisse was a complete surprise to Jasmine. She sat on a stool with a Spanish guitar. She had placed some flowers and a small Spanish comb in her hair. She made a magnificent picture as she poised ready to sing and play. She had chosen *"Cuando Salí de Cuba,"* "When I Left Cuba," an old Spanish favorite. Her voice was deep and husky, curiously attractive although limited in range.

Bill and Paul who came next both apologized for having very little talent to offer. Bill showed a few slides that he had with him of faraway places, and Paul, who claimed that astrology was his hobby, made a hilarious attempt at guessing each person's birth date after asking what he said were pertinent questions. Nobody took him very seriously; in fact he came in for quite a bit of good-natured teasing from the audience.

Étienne sang from *Gigi*—"Thank Heaven for Little Girls" à la Maurice Chevalier.

Jason brought out his pad and drew a quick sketch of each of his guests as they had looked doing their little performances, and finally they all trooped upstairs for Jasmine to play in the music room. She played a selection of Chopin waltzes, her fingers liltingly moving over the keys.

Jason requested that they finish off the evening by gathering around the piano and singing Christmas carols. He sat beside Jasmine while she played, making her feel happy and contented.

CHAPTER SEVEN

Jason and Jasmine were the first up on Christmas morning.

"As soon as we've had a light breakfast, we can go down to the early morning church service in the village," suggested Jason. "I don't expect any of the others will be surfacing before noon."

"Yes," agreed Jasmine, and then added without thinking, "I do hope Paul won't have a hangover." She blushed because it was surely none of her business if one of Jason's friends drank too much. Not that Paul had got really drunk or become offensive—he had quite simply consumed an enormous amount of alcohol.

She was curious. "How did you come to make Paul your agent?"

Jason stared at her. "I guess you mean he's a pretty unlikely character for a promotion manager. In a way, you're right. He's very hard on himself both in work and in play. I think that's what makes him so fantastically good at his job. He never does anything half-heartedly. And don't think that life has been unduly good to him. Believe me, he has more than earned and deserved all he has achieved. He started off life with just about everything and everyone against him. But he preserved, never lost faith in himself. I admire that. Oh, I grant you, he's a rather strange, unruly character, takes a bit of getting used to, but he bears everyone goodwill and he has superb business acumen."

At Jasmine's request they walked down the hill to the church in the village. It had been snowing for some time, large downy flakes softly, slowly falling to earth in a motion as gentle as a sigh. The world around looked polka-dotted, the trees were eagerly extending their branches to receive the white blessing. It was perfect weather for Christmas Day, everything was hushed and still as if in reverence.

When they returned to the house after church, they found everyone else eagerly awaiting them.

"Come on, we're all dying to explore these mysterious packages under the tree," called Paul. They had all piled their various gifts to each other at the foot of the tree the previous evening, and now was the time to open them and wish each other a happy Christmas.

Jasmine had been worried about what to buy for Jason. She never got the opportunity to visit the larger shops in Owen Sound where she might purchase something really nice, so she had puzzled and wondered what she could do that would be both pleasing and original. The perfect idea had come to her as she had been designing the quilt blocks. That was why she had worked so hard and industriously, sometimes way into the wee hours of the morning. It was all for Jason.

The finished product of her loving labors lay now under the tree, carefully wrapped in silver paper and tied with a red ribbon. She had pushed it well back so that it would be one of the last ones opened.

She hadn't forgotten her sister either, and had managed to get Linda to purchase Janice's favorite perfume on one of her visits to Owen Sound.

Their guests had brought gifts for Jason and Jasmine—records and a beautiful vase and a mohair car rug.

Jasmine shyly accepted her gift from Jason. What would it be? She opened the small box to find a gift that quite deprived her of breath for a moment.

"You do like it, don't you?" asked Jason anxiously, possibly misinterpreting her silence.

How could anybody not like the exquisite silver watch with a diamond and emerald band that shone up at her from its bed of white velvet? The emeralds on the band appeared again on the watch face where they marked out the hours.

"It-it's lovely, Jason," she stammered. She hardly knew how to thank him. Never had she seen a more beautifully crafted watch.

She placed her gift to Jason in his hands, hardly daring to hope that he would really like it. She made a wall hanging depicting the sleigh ride they had enjoyed together in the snow, the day when it seemed as if the whole village had joined them in their merriment. The people and the sleigh were sewn in just as she remembered them—and she did recall that day so very vividly. The adults were laughing and singing and the children's faces were alight with joy. How many hours it had taken to craft each feature on each face, the background pale pink for the children and different shades of beige and brown for the adults, the features sewn in single strands of embroidery silk. Each figure was a work of art, carefully and lovingly executed. Mr. Bunty was clearly recognizable at the front holding the reins of the horses that sported an assortment of silver harness bells.

There was a very long silence as Jason stared down at the gift in his hands. When he finally raised his head, his eyes were full of wonder and pride.

"You made this yourself," he said slowly. "I shall treasure it all my life. Jasmine, do you realize how good this is? As a work of art, I mean." He turned to Paul who was even now echoing those very sentiments.

"Things like this are very salable—even when not worked in this professional way. Jasmine, if you wanted, you could have a whole career open up in this."

She was shy and confused, pleased that her work had met with such praise, but overwhelmed by the extent of that praise. She was quite relieved when Jason finally put the wall hanging on one side and she ceased to be the object of such undivided attention.

A relaxed atmosphere pervaded throughout the day. In the afternoon Janice persuaded Jason to take her out on the snowmobile, and Paul and Bob decided to accompany them. It had started to snow again after stopping briefly for a short while at lunchtime, but as there was no wind, it was a perfect day for a snowmobile ride. When they had all gone, Étienne expressed a desire to walk down to the village, and as Clarisse and Bill were very much involved in a game of chess, Jasmine suggested that she accompany him.

They both dressed warmly. Jasmine put on her orange snowmobile suit, as it was the warmest and most comfortable clothing she had. The snow was crisp underfoot. They walked along the side of the road, although there was no traffic, for this was where there was the best foothold.

Étienne obviously loved this kind of weather. While Jasmine tended to hunch up her shoulders and hide her face, he walked with shoulders back and face lifted to allow the snow to fall freely upon him.

"I remember when we were children," he said, "we'd walk for miles in the snow. Schoolbuses were few and far between in those days, certainly in the northern Québec area where I was brought up. We had to walk five miles to school every day, whatever the weather. It was cold and hard going sometimes but we grew to love the winters when each familiar landmark would be transformed into something new and wonderful by the clinging snow or the dripping icicles. Do you have much snow where you come from in England?"

Jasmine laughed. "Hardly a single flake. We often get through a whole winter without any snow at all, and even when it does snow, it just seems to cover the ground briefly and is gone again in a very short time."

"How I would hate that." Étienne lifted his arms to catch the dancing snowflakes. "Winter without snow—certainly Christmas without snow—just wouldn't feel the same."

Jasmine was amused by her companion's boyish appreciation of what was to her no more than an attractive phenomenon. She liked the look of the snow, appreciated the landscape decked like a bride in filmy finery, but she could also see that there were grave disadvantages involved too.

"I don't know how we'd exist in England if we had this much snow," she spoke her thoughts aloud. "Why, we never use snow tires, and have no equipment for clearing away the snow. When on two or three occasions that I can remember we have had a precipitation of four or five inches, everything has been brought to a standstill. Buses couldn't run, cars slid all over the road, old people panicked when they couldn't get out to shop—no, we'd never manage."

"Then you'd need snowmobiles, snowplows, and snowblowers. A whole new industry would start up."

Jasmine was doubtful of the value of that.

"Yes, but just think how many industries would stop. The building of houses goes on throughout the year in England, whereas construction here seems to be at a minimum. And how about road mending and road construction? Can anything like that be continued in these weather conditions?"

Étienne had to admit that she had a point. But she was being too practical, he argued. Where was her romantic spirit? Couldn't she admire the fantastic visual beauty without thinking of the disadvantages?

They reached the village and turned down the main street. It was empty everywhere. They could hear the drone of a snowmobile in the distance, and a lone car passed by them as they trudged down between the snowbanks. Turning the corner, they walked toward the beach and stood there watching the sluggish waves drag themselves to the shore.

"Jason said that all of this would freeze over." Jasmine still found that hard to believe.

"I came here one February and found the whole bay frozen solid and people skating on the ice. It's a wonderful sight, and such a feeling of goodwill envelops everybody in those conditions. You'll see, in a few weeks the snowmobiles will be skimming across this bay right over to the other side where your house is on the cliff."

On their way back to the house the falling snow increased in volume and, as they were walking uphill, they had to slacken their speed, so breathless did they become.

"Hold on to my arm," shouted Étienne as Jasmine slipped and slithered on the treacherous combination of light powdery snow on the slick hardened crust. She complied and they were walking arm in arm, laughing at some silly quip of Étienne's, when Jason, at the porch putting away the snowmobile, noticed their approach. His mouth hardened slightly and his eyes narrowed. Jasmine had the distinct impression that he was not pleased to see her on such easy, friendly terms with Étienne. *Good,* she thought. *A little jealousy wouldn't hurt him, either.*

The guests stayed for another two days and when they had gone, the house was strangely empty and quiet. Janice, of course, was still staying on. She showed no signs of leaving. Jason seemed to enjoy her company and Jasmine had not the heart to suggest that her twin was outstaying her welcome.

As the days went by and turned into weeks, Jasmine did try to broach the subject of her sister's long stay.

"Do you really object to her being here?" Jason asked, eyebrows raised in quizzical surprise, to which she replied haltingly that it wasn't that she minded too much, just that she thought it would be nice to be alone for a while.

Jason looked at her steadily, his gaze seeming to bore into her innermost soul. He seemed to be trying to convey a message to her. Then why didn't he say something? Was it so difficult to talk to her? She thought again what a devastatingly handsome figure he was. His height and build were attractive to begin with, but added to that all his natural charm, his huge green eyes, the cut and cleft of his firm facial features softened by his mobile mouth, made him an exceptionally attractive man. He was someone who would be noticed and admired anywhere. He held himself with a sort of regal bearing that would make him stand out in a crowd, and yet at the same time he showed a sensitivity that dispelled all appearance of arrogance.

As she tried to bear his gaze, Jasmine felt her legs trembling and her senses swooning. She was completely besotted with him, completely under his spell. And yet she was aware that on the occasions when he would come to her at night, although physically she gave herself to him with delight and total abandon, she still held herself partly from him spiritually.

She could not bring herself to a total commitment of mind and body. Not until she resolved the question of Jason's exact feelings for her. Not until they were able to communicate with each other verbally as fully as they seemed to be able to communicate physically.

She could not deny that each moment that she spent in Jason's arms had an aching sweetness about it. She wanted him and needed him so desperately. But what if she wanted more than he was ultimately prepared to give? Sometimes she would look at Jason and Janice as they sat with their heads close together, whispering and laughing, and she would question whether Jason was revealing to her twin the whispered confidences and intimacies that she longed to hear. She had decided long ago that if Jason, contrary to his first disclaimer, eventually asked for a divorce, she would step aside, much as she loved him, and grant him that. But it was becoming increasingly difficult to still believe that. Lately she had felt a growing antagonism that told her that she should not let things progress that far. She should fight for her man in open warfare. Why let him ruin his life? She was sure that there would be no happiness for him with Janice. Was she prepared to let him make such a mistake? Then she would quickly quell the insidious whisper. Jason had a right to decide for himself and she must not listen to the selfish dictates of her own heart.

All these thoughts went through her head as she suffered Jason's piercing stare. Still he looked at her steadily. He seemed about to say something. He had the air of wanting to speak his mind about an important matter. But then he just shrugged his shoulders, half turning from her as he did so.

"Jan's presence doesn't irk me at all. If you want her to go, I think you should tell her so yourself. After all, you are mistress of this house, you know."

She was left deflated and tonguetied. So Janice's presence didn't irk him? She bet it didn't. He wanted to have his cake and eat it too!

That night Jasmine was almost too dispirited to join in the conversation, so she just sat back and listened. Janice was claiming all Jason's attention anyway. She was full of ideas for a planned trip to Toronto. She had persuaded Jason to take her so that she could do some more shopping. Jasmine had been urged to go, too, by Jason, that is—but the way she felt right now she didn't know if she would go or not.

As Jason and Janice talked, completely oblivious of her presence, Jasmine decided to go upstairs and wash her hair, and then probably go to bed early. Just when she had thought that Jason and she were beginning to really appreciate each other, everything had suddenly gone wrong. She couldn't understand it.

After she had bathed and washed and dried her hair, she decided she would like to read for a while before going to sleep. But she had no book in her room that she had not already read. She slipped into a negligee and tiptoed downstairs, thinking that perhaps the other two had already retired. There was nobody in the lounge, but as she went toward the library she detected a light and could hear the sound of voices through the partly open door. She hesitated, wondering whether to still choose a book or whether to forget the idea. As she paused, the voices rose and clearly came to her ears. She hadn't in truth meant to eavesdrop, but that is what happened.

Janice's voice was loud and strident. "Why does she always have to spoil everything? I don't believe you really care about her and yet she comes between us all the time."

Jason's response was too low for her to hear, but Janice continued, "Just why did you marry her, Jason? You really can't love a mousy little creature like her. Darling, you could have had me. Why didn't you wait a bit longer?"

Jason's reply was largely indistinct, but Jasmine caught a few phrases, among which clearly came out, ". . . should have waited."

She didn't wait to hear more. She didn't want to know what else he had to say. She turned and raced up the stairs. As she came to the top and made for her door, she glanced down and saw that Jason had come out of the library and was now standing in the lounge looking up at her.

He knew she had heard. She didn't stop. She reached the safety of her room, closed the door, and put out the light. She got into bed and pulled the sheets up tight, knowing with certainty that Jason would come.

He did come. He put on the light as he came over to the bed and sat down on the edge.

"Jasmine."

"Go away! I don't want to listen!"

Jason pulled the sheets away from her face and forced her to turn and look at him. When persuasion failed, he resorted to brute strength.

"Just how much did you hear?"

"Enough!"

"Enough for you to get completely the wrong impression. You can't have heard all I said or you wouldn't be upset."

"Is that so? Well, let me tell you what I heard." She was hurt enough and mad enough to want to throw his words back in his face. She couldn't stand the way he was looking at her with such tender compassion. He didn't have to feel so sorry just because he couldn't love her. What did she care? If he had been honest with her from the start, none of this would have happened. "I heard you say that you wish you had waited before you had married me."

"And?"

"Well, isn't that enough? Do you mean to tell me there's more?"

"Jasmine, you heard an isolated phrase. You should have heard the rest."

"Can you deny that you said that?"

"No." His voice was almost inaudible.

"And did you mean it?"

"Jasmine, I said other things."

"*Did you mean it?*"

Jason sighed. He stood up and moved away from the bed, then turned back in resignation.

"In a way it's true. No, Jasmine, this part you'll have to hear. Things didn't turn out at all as planned and I began to regret our hasty marriage, *but not for the reasons you're thinking.* I was almost getting to the stage where I thought we could talk it out together, and then this had to happen. We're farther apart than before. Please, Jasmine, please, just trust me."

Trust him! When he had gone, Jasmine tried to sort out her jumbled thoughts. She wanted to trust him—heaven knew she wanted to trust him. *Then why don't you?* said a little voice inside her. She pondered the question. Just why wouldn't she trust him? The answer came back to her immediately, as though it had been lurking in her heart for a long time just waiting to be discovered. It was herself she didn't trust. How could she believe that a shy, unspectacular creature like herself could ever attract and hold a man like Jason? Didn't she know that her only hold on him was her resemblance to Janice? On the other hand, if she trusted him, she would surely not believe him capable of such empty affection. Did she think he had no intelligence or integrity? She came to the startling conclusion that if she were to trust him, then she would also have to believe in herself. This knowledge made her lighthearted. It was as if her belief in Jason strengthened her ability to believe in herself.

Strangely enough, she slept well that night and the next morning she was able to face Jason over the breakfast table with clear eyes and an open smile. She had dressed with care. She was determined to give Janice a run for her money. *Remember,* she kept telling herself, *you believe in yourself too.* She wore a pink sherbet woolen dress, with a wide puritan-style white satin collar. The color enhanced the creaminess of her skin and she knew she looked good.

Jason looked good too. He wore dark green corduroy slacks with a lighter green turtle neck sweater. His hair shone softly and the wisps escaping over his forehead smoothed out the angles of his face.

Jasmine knew that her husband's eyes were on her, carefully assessing how she was reacting to the events of the previous night. So she talked quite naturally about their planned trip to Toronto, mentioning a few things she would like to see, a play she had read a good review of, a concert she would like to attend. As she talked, she felt Jason relax.

She planned another wall hanging that day, working solidly in her room. She wanted to have an idea of what materials and supplies she would purchase in Toronto.

CHAPTER EIGHT

It was a perfect day for a flight, cold but clear. For once Janice made the effort of getting up early, so they all breakfasted together and were able to set off before ten o'clock. As the airplane gathered speed along the runway and climbed into the sky, Jasmine could feel her spirits lifting. They soared like a bird, detached from the world. Far below they could see the earth covered with its white blanket. They seemed to have had less snow in Lion's Head than in the stretch of country between Owen Sound and Toronto. Was that possible? She found it hard to believe how even more snow could have fallen in other areas.

"That's the snow belt we're passing over," explained Jason. "They're glad of the snow, believe me, for their skiing is a multimillion-dollar enterprise."

If she really looked more carefully, Jasmine could see signs of ski tracks and ski lifts on the hillsides. The rolling hills were dotted with Swiss-style chalets, but there the resemblance to Switzerland ended, for the Canadian countryside here had a softer quality, the hills rolling instead of rugged.

Farther south toward Toronto there were only smatterings of snow and the exposed grass had a distinctly greener appearance than in the north. This time Jason planned to land the little plane at Toronto International Airport, so he was in touch with the tower, waiting his turn to land. They circled while a large 747 came in. It was frightening to Jasmine to think that these monsters were in the air with them and she was relieved when it was their turn and they touched down and taxied off out of the way.

"We'll take a taxi to my apartment first of all," said Jason. "You'll have two or three days to do your shopping or whatever it is that you want to do. But I must be back home by the weekend."

This was the first that Jasmine had heard about an apartment, though it seemed to come as no surprise to Janice. She sighed. There were still a lot of things she didn't know about Jason.

The apartment was situated in downtown Toronto in Bay Street. Apparently there weren't too many apartments available that were as centrally situated as this one, so Jason was anxious to hold on to it even though he did not use it very much.

"It has the advantage of being centrally located and yet is in a safe area, both in the daytime and in the evening. That's not to say that you two girls can go and come as you please at all hours of the day and night," warned Jason. "I want to know where you are, and if you're out after dark you must return in a taxi. There are no exceptions to that rule."

"Good heavens," shuddered Jasmine, "you make me feel as if I am in gangster country."

"No, no, nothing as bad as that. Toronto is one of the safest North American cities, though we have had some trouble in recent months. I don't want to alarm you, but I do want you to be careful."

The elevator took them up to the apartment on the fourth floor. It was a small apartment, though beautifully furnished. It consisted of a large lounge, two bedrooms, bathroom, and small kitchenette. The three full-length windows in the lounge overlooked a medley of buildings and between them could be seen the banana-shaped curves of City Hall.

Janice flung herself into a chair.

"Lord, I'm hungry. Getting up early always makes me feel famished by lunchtime. Let's send out for something, Jason."

"I'll put some coffee on," volunteered Jason. "We can unpack first and then decide about lunch. I have an appointment today and I'll have to make a phone call before I know about lunch." He waved toward the bedrooms. "Ours is the one on the right, Jasmine."

Jasmine took her valise and opened it on the bed. The room was larger than she had expected. It, too, overlooked the same view as the lounge. There was a large double bed in the center of the far wall, and two large wardrobes as well as a dressing table, a TV, and two easy chairs. The cover of the bed was shining orange satin as were the curtains, while the carpet was a cream shag.

She hadn't brought many dresses. She unpacked her belongings and laid them on the bed while she went to place her toiletries on the dressing table. Then she went over to one of the big wardrobes. She was just opening the doors to put her dresses inside when Jason appeared. She turned to look at him as he entered and so it was that she saw the frozen expression on his face as he gazed past her into the wardrobe she had opened to reveal a host of frilly dresses, nightgowns, and other feminine articles. Jason thrust her aside almost roughly as he grabbed the offending clothes, calling, "Janice! Janice! Come here!"

His face was white, his lips frozen into a tight line. As Janice entered, he threw the clothes at her.

"Get these things out of here! And would you mind explaining to us just how they got here?"

Janice seemed to be covered in confusion. With just the right hint of delicate coverup she said, looking at Jason from under her long lashes, "Explain? How? Oh! I see! Yes, well, of course they're left over from my shopping trip to Toronto before Christmas. I took the liberty of sleeping in this room. I hope you don't mind."

Jason's face was expressionless, immobile, save for a nerve that twitched in his jaw.

"Just get them out of here." He turned away to the window.

Janice flashed Jasmine a smirk of triumph as she left the room.

Throughout all this Jasmine had stood as though paralyzed, unable to move. Her eyes had gazed from Jason's livid countenance to Janice's scarcely flustered simpering coyness.

She looked now at Jason's back as he stood at the window. Was he mad because Janice had played an underhanded trick, guaranteed to cause trouble or, at the very least, sow seeds of doubt in Jasmine's mind? Or was he mad for another reason?

He turned slowly to meet her tortured gaze.

"Jasmine, I . . ."

The shrill of the telephone interrupted and as he went to answer it Jasmine could see that all thoughts of their problem were dismissed from his mind as he discussed business details with the caller.

He replaced the phone. "Jasmine, I have to leave. I'll be back later today and we can talk then."

He handed her a key and some notes, reminding her to be careful and not to be out after dark if possible.

When he had gone, Jasmine put away her clothes and then unpacked Jason's things too. She went into the kitchenette to examine the food situation. There was a large refrigerator and a small deep-freeze. It was clear that somebody had brought in provisions for them. There was bread, butter, milk, cheese, and a variety of cooked meats, pies, and vegetables. In the wall cupboards were canned goods, cereals, coffee, and sugar.

There was surely no need to send out for food as Janice had suggested.

Jasmine was busy frying bacon and eggs and toasting some bread when Janice appeared on the scene.

"Don't fix anything for me. I'm going to eat out." She smiled sweetly at Jasmine. "I told you that you would only get hurt if you persisted. Jason's a real flesh-and-blood man. He needs more than a pale shadow of a woman."

It was a pity that the day which had started off so

well had now been spoiled. It was very hard for Jasmine to remain cheerful and unaffected by her twin's vindictiveness. She decided to forget her problems by going shopping. Jason had explained to her that many large stores were within a stone's throw of his apartment. There was the new and very modern Eaton Centre, a complex of all sorts of shops located in a big mall.

She dressed in a green leather coat that had been one of Jason's purchases for her before their wedding and green boots to match. A white mohair beret and scarf completed the outfit.

It took her only a few minutes to reach the Eaton Centre. The front of the multistory building faced out into the merging of two streets like the prow of a ship. This front section was entirely made of glass in a very modern concept and design so that all the different levels were exposed to view.

Inside there were goods of every description from all countries of the world, it seemed. Jasmine spent so long browsing through the clothes, the shoes, the book department, the imported furniture section, that the day passed very quickly and she still had not even started to look at the small boutiques that made up the rest of the mall.

She made her way to the fabric department and spent the next hour choosing materials, picking them for their color and texture, buying small amounts of each so that she would have a wide variety to choose from when she got home.

As she was leaving the store, her arms full of packages, a familiar voice called her name and, turning quickly, she saw that Étienne was hurrying after her.

"What a surprise seeing you here! I thought you would still be in the wilds of Lion's Head. Good heavens, you seem to have bought up the whole of the Eaton Centre," he exclaimed, cheerfully unburdening her of her parcels and loading himself up with them. "I guess you're making for the apartment with this lot?"

She nodded, speechless at the way he had arrived like a whirlwind and taken over everything. He turned with her out of the Centre and in the direction of Jason's apartment.

"Lucky you saw me," he said. "I know it's not far, but all this is too much for you to carry."

They reached the apartment and Étienne carried her purchases inside. Nobody was home. Jasmine had expected Jason to be back, for it was nearly six o'clock.

There was a note on the coffee table. "Gone out again. Won't be back till late." It was signed Jason and Janice.

Jasmine bit her lip. Did they have to make it so obvious that she was not wanted? Étienne was watching her from the door.

"Why don't you come to the theater with me? I have complimentary tickets for the opening night of *The Heiress* at the O'Keefe Centre." Seeing her hesitation, he added quickly, "You surely don't want to spend the evening alone. I promise to see you safely back to the door."

Jasmine added her own little explanation underneath Jason's—Gone with Étienne to the O'Keefe.

"I can make us supper if you like," she suggested, but Étienne shook his head.

"Let's go somewhere special. You look as if you need cheering up. Most women blossom after marriage, but you are looking a little peaked." He then added astutely, "Has our little feline friend been getting to you?"

As she colored, he was quick to apologize. "Sorry, I guess I shouldn't have said that. After all, she is your sister."

Jasmine said thoughtfully, "It's strange you don't like her. All men do. It's usually the women who can't stand her."

Étienne chuckled. "I can well imagine."

"Will you give me a moment to change?" Jasmine had heard that theatergoers at the O'Keefe usually wore evening dress, and she didn't want to be out of place. It only took her a minute or two and then she was standing in the doorway wearing a long creamy woolen dress, bronze sandals, and fur coat. Étienne approved her choice with gleaming eyes as they went down in the elevator to hail a taxi.

The restaurant Étienne had chosen was not too far away. It was called the Talk of the Town and it featured a very plush decor. As soon as they were seated at a table spaced nicely distant from the neighboring ones, Étienne ordered a pre-dinner drink for each of them.

"What will you have to eat?" he asked, handing her the menu. The variety of dishes was such that it was difficult to make a choice, but she eventually chose the Cornish hen Rossini.

"Good! And let's have minestrone soup to start."

It was a delicious meal, beautifully and tastefully served. The Cornish hen was cooked in a Madeira wine sauce and was utterly delicious. After baba au rhum they both enjoyed coffee. Jasmine found that the atmosphere, the change from the countryside of Lion's Head, the animation and bustle of the town, all had contributed to cheer her up. She was grateful to Étienne for seeing her need and treating her to this evening. She sensed that he had guessed that all was not well in her world at the moment, but he was too discreet to do more than hint at his suspicions. She was grateful for that, too, though whether his thoughtfulness was prompted by his friendship and loyalty to Jason or his liking and sympathy for her she did not know.

The play began at eight o'clock, and by the time they had arrived at the O'Keefe, so had many others. Jasmine was glad that she had thought to wear an evening dress because as more and more patrons entered the foyer, she realized hardly anyone was in a short skirt. The large entrance foyer at the O'Keefe was like the interior of some huge ballroom, only the floor was carpeted. At the center back rose a wide curving staircase leading to the upper circles of the theater. The men were in evening jackets and fancy shirts and dark trousers, the women in gorgeous finery and flashing jewels. The animated and excited conversation of people who anticipated an enjoyable evening was intoxicating to Jasmine.

They had splendid seats in the orchestra. Étienne explained that as a theater critic he was always given complimentary tickets for opening nights.

The play *The Heiress* was a very dramatic story—the bitter account of a young girl, shy to the point of gaucheness, who had grown up in the shadow of her dead mother's wit and charm, always struggling to replace the gay, vibrant young wife her father had lost. But her father considered her only charm to be the large fortune he would leave her on his death. Nevertheless, he shields her from all fortune hunters. One man woos her and wins her heart, delights her, makes her feel charming and witty and gay, but her father cruelly exposes him as a fortune hunter. She loves him to the end, but when he returns after her father's death, she leads him on just so that she can have the pleasure of crushing his rising hopes.

Jasmine was enthralled throughout; the ornate decor, the lavish costuming, and the pathetically sad story of revenge held her interest till the final curtain.

It was late when the taxi deposited them outside Jason's apartment. Étienne instructed the driver to wait while he escorted her up to the apartment door.

"I won't come in. It's too late. I'll probably see you again before you go back to Lion's Head. We could all have a drink and a meal together one evening. I'll be in touch with Jason."

"Thank you for a wonderful evening." She hadn't enjoyed herself so much in a long time.

"You're very welcome, Jasmine." He smiled, affectionately touched her cheek, and was gone.

Jason was still up, pacing back and forth in the

living room. Upon Jasmine's entrance, he turned quickly.

"Where on earth have you been? I was worried about you. After what I said to you this morning I can only assume that you stayed out late without any indication as to where you were in order to cause me pain."

She was surprised, off guard. "B-but I left you a note, Jason. I told you I was going to the O'Keefe Centre with Étienne and would be safe with him."

Jason's eyes narrowed. "If you did leave me a note, where is it?"

"Why, on the end of yours, of course. I used the same paper, thinking that a message would be most noticeable there."

Jason looked skeptical. "Really? Here's the note you speak of." He handed her the paper. She read it through and then looked up at him.

"But, Jason, my note's not here."

"Precisely what I was trying to tell you, my dear. Now, how about thinking up a better story?"

She felt her anger rising within her. How dare he doubt her! After the nonsense she had to put up with this morning, the way he had rushed off, explanations forgotten, her sister's sneering remarks—all this had been endured without a word of censure, and now, at the first small sign of a misdemeanor from her, he was condemning her and taunting her.

"There *was* a note there, Jason, but it has been torn off. When I came back to the apartment with Étienne —he had seen me struggling with my parcels in the store and kindly helped me—we found your note on the table, but it had Janice's name on it, too." She looked again at the note. "See, just where the note ends. You can see the beginning of some more writing. I thought you and Janice had gone out together, and when Étienne invited me to the theater I didn't think you'd mind."

Jason was beginning to look slightly mollified. "But who tore off the note? Are you absolutely sure that you wrote on the same paper?"

Jasmine knew only too well.

"Forget it, Jason. It's just another of those funny little things that have been happening lately. I think I'll go to bed now." She turned at the bedroom door. "I'm sorry you had to be so worried, but you needn't have been. I wouldn't do anything to alarm you."

Much later she heard Janice return, and an angry exchange ensued between her and Jason.

The next day Jasmine made her way to the art gallery where she knew Jason's paintings were on show. He had not offered to take her; she knew that he had another business appointment that day and so she decided to go herself in case she didn't get another opportunity.

A quiet atmosphere pervaded the gallery. There were several rooms of paintings, each one featuring the works of a different Canadian artist. She wandered around the other rooms first, deliberately leaving Jason's paintings to savor last. She examined not only the paintings but also the reactions of the visitors.

When she finally came to her husband's room, she noticed with pleasure and a feeling of humble pride that here there were more people. Their comments seemed very favorable. She had already seen some of the paintings, but there were also many that were new to her. Two or three delighted her particularly, revealing as they did a new facet of Jason's character.

He had a section of paintings of children depicted in various attitudes. One showed a little red-haired girl sitting in a field of flowers and studiously examining a daisy with an expression of childlike rapture on her face. Another showed a familiar scene—a sleigh pulled by two horses through a village street, with the snow pelting down and a crowd of laughing, happy people riding, while two or three children ran alongside throwing snowballs.

It was apparent that the artist was a man of feeling and sensitivity. One look at his canvases revealed that here was a man who saw with his heart, not his eyes.

Coming upon the next canvas, Jasmine gasped in wonder. This was a portrait of her sitting in the music room at the baby grand. She had a faraway expression in her eyes, and as she played, a small boy of about two sat at her feet and played with a pile of building blocks. His head was turned away so that his face was not visible, but Jasmine had the definite feeling that at any moment he would turn his head and smile and his baby face would be a childlike replica of Jason's.

The painting was creating quite a stir, and as she stood with the crowd and drank in every detail, she found herself wanting to possess the painting so badly that over and over again her mind kept saying,

180

Don't let this one be sold. Don't let it be sold. A vain hope it appeared, for there were many interested comments, and several people looked at the price tag. Jasmine didn't even want to know how much it was; she knew it would be mindboggling, but as far as she was concerned the painting was priceless.

At that moment one of the admirers exclaimed in awe, "Why, you're the girl in the painting. You must know the artist." She was immediately surrounded by people, all delightedly reiterating how good a likeness the artist had captured.

A group of people came across from the far end of the room and a hand grasped her arm and Jason's voice said, "Jasmine! I didn't know you were coming here today. Come on, I want you to meet some friends of mine." So saying, he smiled nicely at the crowd, apologized for dragging her away, and neatly extricated her.

"Why didn't you tell me you were coming?" he asked as he bore her off. "I would have been here to meet you."

"I didn't want to bother you. You seemed so busy with all your business appointments. Besides, I enjoyed coming alone," she assured him. She glanced back at the painting that she had been admiring. "Jason, that painting, I—I . . ."

"Yes?" He smiled down at her. "You like it?"

"Oh, yes! Yes, I do. But—" How could she tell him that she wanted it for herself? That if ever there came a time when Janice's schemes won out, and the only man she could ever love disappeared from her life, she would have the painting to cherish; she would forever imagine that that faceless child would turn around, and she would see what it would have been like to have had Jason's son. "Jason, you won't sell that painting, will you?"

"I've a feeling it may be already sold."

Her disappointment was hard to contain, but Jason was leading her across the room to where Paul stood with two distinguished-looking gentlemen. He introduced her as his wife, and they immediately told her how pleased they were to meet the woman of the two paintings.

"*Two* paintings?"

Jason pointed to the far end of the room where the Orpheus canvas was displayed to advantage.

"Oh!" She wanted to say that they were wrong, that Eurydice had been painted of her sister, but how were they to know about Janice? Wouldn't they find it strange that the artist had not depicted his wife in such an evocative painting? She just smiled and nodded.

She left Jason at the art gallery, declining to have lunch with him, making the excuse that she had seen a dress that she wanted to buy before somebody else fell in love with it. It seemed a flimsy excuse to her, but Jason seemed satisfied with it. Did he not know that she'd rather be with him than do anything else in the world? She had refused because she thought she would be in the way of the business dealings.

When she arrived back at the apartment, she felt very depressed. Seeing Jason in his world with his friends, seeing the fantastic adulation given to his paintings by the Canadian public, made her realize that he was one man in a million. How fantastic he had looked today, dressed in a dark-blue suit with a fitted waist and semi-flared jacket. His shirt had ruffles at the sleeves and down the front, while at the neck had been tied a blue velvet bow tie. How desperately she loved him. How much she wanted to spend all her life with him. What would it be like to have his whole confidence, to listen to the whispering of his secret plans and dreams? She knew she would be content with nothing less.

Janice made an appearance just as Jasmine was preparing a salad and cold meat for lunch. No doubt the smell of the freshly perked coffee had awoken her and brought her forth. She was still dressed in her nightgown and negligee. She sat down at the kitchen table and poured herself a cup of coffee, yawning and stretching luxuriously.

Jasmine asked her if she would like some salad for lunch. Her sister stared vindictively at her from under half-closed lashes.

"Honestly, Jas, you never give up being sweet, do you? I get so sick of that. The time has come for you and me to have a showdown."

"I don't know what you mean." Jasmine's first reaction was to try and avoid a fight, but her sister persisted.

"Come off it, Jasmine. You know what I mean. Jason is *my property.* You took my man and now you're paying for it. Honey, I know you think you're in love with him, but face the truth. It's me he loves, me he wanted to marry, but he just couldn't wait for me to come back on my terms and he married you instead in a fit of depression and despair. Do you really want him under those conditions?"

Jasmine searched for the right words. She didn't know how to react to Janice's words because she didn't know to what extent they were true. Jason had never admitted his love for Janice. He had talked only of a bargain. She took a deep breath.

"You're trying to bluff me, Jan."

"No, I'm not. And what's more, I was trying to save your face. But you're so stupid you can't see that, can you? Don't you know that Jason and I were lovers? Oh, yes! Don't flinch. Don't look so disgusted. We're not all the prude that you are. How do you suppose it feels to him to make love to you? Don't blush. I know he's been in your bed, and I'm rather afraid that I sent him there. You see, I told him that there would be nothing more between us till he had divorced you. What a quandary that put him in." She laughed. "You can't imagine what fun it was to lead him on, flirt with him, and then dash water in his face. How many times he must have come to you just to forget his need for me."

"Stop!" cried Jasmine. "I don't want to hear any more. You're lying. Jason wouldn't do that." Jasmine covered her ears and put her head down on the kitchen table and wept.

Janice stood up and offered one last parting shot. "So you see, my dear, I effectively stopped any romance between the two of you. You know what an honorable man Jason is. Can you imagine how he must hate himself for making use of you as he has?"

It was sometime later that Jasmine decided to go

back to Lion's Head. She didn't want to stay in Toronto any longer. She might enjoy Jason's company, but the constant presence of her twin was more than she could take, and in view of the latest accusations, she had to be alone to consider the problem. She decided that she would pack her clothes and rent a car to drive back to Lion's Head.

She left a note for Jason in the bedroom where, hopefully, Janice would not be able to tamper with it, and then went down in the elevator to the ground floor. As she stepped out into the street, she almost cannoned into a figure hurrying into the building.

"Jasmine!" She would rather have got away without seeing him.

"I-I want to return to Lion's Head. I left you a note upstairs. I didn't think you'd object to my driving myself back there."

"Oh, but I do object. In the first place, I expect my wife to report to me personally before rushing off. And, secondly, I object to your driving in such bad weather conditions. If you wanted so badly to return home, why didn't you ask me to fly you back? After all, it's my privilege as your husband to look after you."

He was right and she was ashamed. "I'm sorry, I just didn't want to bother you."

Jason glanced at his watch. They were still standing outside the apartment building.

"Look, let's go and have something to eat and then I'll fly you back home."

He took her to the Chat Doré—an unpretentious French restaurant where they had steaming French-

185

Canadian green pea soup and crusty French bread. He didn't try to question her or pry into her reasons for wanting to return home so suddenly.

"I'm afraid I'm being a big nuisance to you, Jason."

"You could never be a nuisance—when are you going to believe that? I just wish I could have had more time to spend with you during the last few weeks, but what with getting ready for this showing of my paintings—it's one of the biggest I've had, to date—and the rush of Christmas, and a host of other things I had to do, I just didn't have the time I would rather have given to you."

It was the nearest thing she had ever heard to a declaration of love. It wasn't much, but it would do for the moment. She herself was suffering from doubts and insecurity, but she also sensed now for the first time that in some way Jason was just as uncertain of her feelings for him. And dear Janice wasn't helping matters.

"Should I go home, Jason?" she asked him.

"Jasmine, I can't advise you about that. You must decide that for yourself. But I'll go along with whatever you decide—about anything."

She hoped he would, for suddenly she knew what she was going to do. As he sat across the table from her, his large green eyes seriously studying her, she knew that she wanted absolutely nothing else in this life but the handsome, distinguished man she had married. Why had she been so fainthearted before? Why had she been so ready to accept defeat and hand him over to Janice? He was one man in a million. He had pledged himself to her. What had he said to her on their wedding night? "Till death us do part." And she had been ready to reject him?

"You needn't fly me home after all," she said. "Take me back to the apartment, please. I have something that must be done without delay."

When they entered the apartment, Janice was sitting flicking through a fashion magazine. Jason hung back in the hallway so Janice did not see him at first. When she glanced up and saw Jasmine with her suitcase, she was quick to comment, "Good! I see you're leaving!"

"No, I'm not, Jan. But you are."

"You're crazy, Jas," sneered her sister.

"No, I'm not. But I must have been crazy to have put up with your poisonous remarks for so long. You see, I love Jason. I love him more than life itself—in fact there would be no meaning or purpose to my life if I couldn't spend it with him. That's why I'm kicking you out. I want him to myself without you constantly hanging around."

"You have no right to throw me out. Wait till Jason hears of this."

"On the contrary, I have every right. By virtue of being Jason's wife, this is my apartment, and I can reject as well as choose my guests."

Jason entered the room, and Janice, casting a furious glance in Jasmine's direction, went into her room and slammed the door.

Jasmine hardly dared look at Jason, but when she did, she saw that his eyes were shining and full of love.

"My darling little spitfire! How I have longed for you to send her packing."

Jasmine could scarcely believe her ears. "Do you mean to say you've been waiting for me to do that? But why didn't you do it yourself if you felt that way?"

"Oh, my love. For a variety of reasons and all of them seem stupid and unimportant now." He kissed her. "I didn't mean for you to make the first declaration of love like that. . . . Do you really love me that much?"

She nodded mutely.

"I don't deserve you, Jasmine. Oh, I've been so foolish. You see, I have always been so uncertain about those I love. I had to be sure that if you loved me, you also loved me enough to fight for me. I wanted you to stand up against Janice and tell her once and for all that you were going after what you really wanted. I knew Janice was coming back from Toronto. I had known where she was all the time. But when you walked in that stormy night, I knew immediately that you were the one and only girl for me."

"But why didn't you just tell me so?"

"I was going to, and then that night when we sat down and talked to each other, I mean really talked . . ."

"Yes, when you told me about your lonely childhood."

"Yes. Well, I realized then that you had a giant-size inferiority complex about Janice and I thought I'd have to be more subtle. If Janice came back before we were married, I was sure it would be my mother's story all over again, with you never even letting yourself become fond of me, let alone conquering your feelings of not counting for much. So I hurried you into marriage and hoped that everything would work out."

"Oh, Jason. It so very nearly didn't." Jasmine shuddered to think how nearly she had left a clear field for Janice.

"I know. I died a thousand deaths believing that I had set too difficult a task for you. And I thought I would lose you forever, just like my mother lost the one she loved. Did you know about that? Did Mrs. Bunty tell you the whole story of how my mother loved another man but her twin sister came and took him away? My mother just shriveled up and died inside. I don't think I ever knew her happy. She married my father as second best—and he knew that too—but she never got over her first love. She would sit at that piano and play for hours on end, that haunting melody from 'Orpheus,' and her thoughts and her heart would be far away."

"How I must have hurt you by playing it so often. But I was so unhappy because I thought you loved Janice and not me."

"You should have known I loved you just by looking at the painting of *Orpheus in the Underworld.*"

Jasmine blushed. "I thought you had painted Jan. I felt sure you must love her very much because you had made her look so soft and breathlessly lovely."

"Just like you're looking now." Jason kissed her lingeringly. "You silly little goose. Janice could never look like that in a thousand years. She has a pinched, mercenary look about her. No, it was you. I must admit that the painting had been finished for some time, all except for the face of Eurydice. That night, when you fell in my arms out of the snow-storm, I stayed up all night and finished it."

They were interrupted by the sound of Janice stomping out of the apartment carrying her valises.

"She tried to tell me you were lovers," said Jasmine unhappily. "I couldn't bear to think that I was second best."

"Oh, my darling! We were never that. You were never second best." Jason got up from the table and took her hand, pulling her to her feet. "Do you realize that we're alone at last? Come."

Much later Jason raised his flushed face and gazed into her eyes.

"That painting you liked so much. It wasn't for sale. We'll hang it in our bedroom where it will witness our dreams come true."

Love—the way you want it!

Candlelight Romances

At your local bookstore or use this handy coupon for ordering:

Dell Bestsellers

- [ ] RANDOM WINDS by Belva Plain $3.50 (17158-X)
- [ ] MEN IN LOVE by Nancy Friday $3.50 (15404-9)
- [ ] JAILBIRD by Kurt Vonnegut $3.25 (15447-2)
- [ ] LOVE: Poems by Danielle Steel $2.50 (15377-8)
- [ ] SHOGUN by James Clavell $3.50 (17800-2)
- [ ] WILL by G. Gordon Liddy $3.50 (09666-9)
- [ ] THE ESTABLISHMENT by Howard Fast.......$3.25 (12296-1)
- [ ] LIGHT OF LOVE by Barbara Cartland $2.50 (15402-2)
- [ ] SERPENTINE by Thomas Thompson $3.50 (17611-5)
- [ ] MY MOTHER/MY SELF by Nancy Friday $3.25 (15663-7)
- [ ] EVERGREEN by Belva Plain $3.50 (13278-9)
- [ ] THE WINDSOR STORY
      by J. Bryan III & Charles J.V. Murphy $3.75 (19346-X)
- [ ] THE PROUD HUNTER by Marianne Harvey ..$3.25 (17098-2)
- [ ] HIT ME WITH A RAINBOW
      by James Kirkwood $3.25 (13622-9)
- [ ] MIDNIGHT MOVIES by David Kaufelt $2.75 (15728-5)
- [ ] THE DEBRIEFING by Robert Litell $2.75 (01873-5)
- [ ] SHAMAN'S DAUGHTER by Nan Salerno
      & Rosamond Vanderburgh $3.25 (17863-0)
- [ ] WOMAN OF TEXAS by R.T. Stevens $2.95 (19555-1)
- [ ] DEVIL'S LOVE by Lane Harris $2.95 (11915-4)

At your local bookstore or use this handy coupon for ordering:

 DELL BOOKS
P.O. BOX 1000, PINEBROOK, N.J. 07058

Please send me the books I have checked above. I am enclosing $_____
(please add 75¢ per copy to cover postage and handling). Send check or money
order—no cash or C.O.D.'s. Please allow up to 8 weeks for shipment.

Mr/Mrs/Miss _____

Address _____

City _____ State/Zip _____